LAKEHOUSE SECRETS

JODI ALLEN VAUGHN

Copyright © 2022 by Jodi Allen Vaughn

All rights reserved.

No part of this book may be reproduced in any form or by any electronic or mechanical means, including information storage and retrieval systems, without written permission from the author, except for the use of brief quotations in a book review.

❀ Created with Vellum

CHAPTER 1

*H*annah Reece wiped down her quartz countertops and carefully placed her pink coffee cup into her Bosch dishwasher and hit the start button.

She walked over to her large picture window over-looking the lake. The sun was just coming up, casting its warm light on the new blanket of snow they'd received during the night. With Thanksgiving behind her, she had to start focusing on Christmas.

The holiday had always been her favorite until James passed away. Now, she wasn't sure the magical day would be the same without her husband.

She smiled as she thought about the last Christmas they had together. James had heard about a widowed father who'd lost his wife in a car accident. His name was Alex Mitchell. He was left with four children all under the age of five to raise on his own. James imme-diately told her to get her coat. They went to the store and bought toys and clothes for the children They had them wrapped and delivered to the Mitchell house the night before Christmas. James insisted they keep it anonymous. They hadn't even told their children what they had done. In addition to the gifts, James had set up college funds for each of the children. He told Hannah it was one less thing for Alex Mitchell to worry about.

It had made the local news and to this day no one knew who the Secret Santa had been.

Except her.

Hannah sighed and glanced at the time. It was a little after six, not too early to visit her friend Carolina Johnson.

Carolina was an early riser, like herself, and would already be up by now.

Since Carolina had moved into the lake house on Laurel Cove, they'd become friends in a short amount of time. While they were both single, she a widow, and Carolina divorced, they quickly discovered they had a lot in common.

Hannah had offered to come over and help Carolina get started on painting the inside of her house. Hannah had loved to paint when her children were young, always painting and decorating their rooms when a new idea or the latest trend hit. Since her kids were grown and had moved away, she found herself lonely and looked for opportunities to get out of the house and keep busy.

Hannah grabbed her goose-down coat and slid it on. She shoved her hands into her gloves, put the fur-lined hood over her head, wrapped the scarf around her neck, and grabbed her house keys.

Despite the freezing temperatures, she felt like walking over to Carolina's instead of driving.

After locking the house she walked in the direction of her neighbor's house.

Hannah had always thought there was something calming about an early morning walk in the snow. The world was quieter and she could just enjoy the beauty of the morning.

Her boots sunk into the white powder with each step she took. The cold air stung her lungs with each inhale.

She made good time and was ringing Carolina's doorbell a few minutes later.

Hannah immediately heard Phoenix barking on the other side and smiled to herself.

Maybe she needed to get a dog, so she wouldn't feel so lonely.

The door swung open and Carolina stood there wearing a large black garbage bag over her clothes. She'd cut out three holes for her arms and head.

"What are you wearing?" Hannah grinned and stepped inside the warmth of the lake house.

While it wasn't as elaborate as her own elegant log cabin, Carolina's house was cozy.

"Don't look at me like that. It's brilliant." Carolina held out her arms and smiled. "I saw this idea on Pinterest. You put a large garbage bag on to protect your clothes while painting."

She smiled at her friend. Since getting divorced, Carolina had been carefully watching every penny and made do with what she had.

Though she'd never been in that financial situation, she admired her friend for how she'd built her life back on her own, without the help of a man. When Carolina wasn't working at the Green Thumb Nursery in town, she was constantly renovating her lake house.

Hannah smiled. "Do you have one in my size?"

Carolina laughed. "Thankfully, it's one-size-fits-all. Although we might have to tie a rope around the waist so it doesn't swallow you. Come on in." She stepped back so Hannah could enter.

The scent of cinnamon and vanilla wrapped around Hannah like a fragrant hug. "Smells wonderful in here."

Carolina grinned. "I made some Christmas cookies this morning. I figured we could have some with our coffee."

Hannah shook her head. "Baking already? You've had a more productive morning than me."

Carolina sighed and walked into the living room with her. "Not by choice. Phoenix was barking his head off this morning. He spotted some deer in the backyard and he wouldn't stop barking until I let him out. Since I was up, I figured I would bake."

Hannah nodded. "All this cold weather has the deer on the move. I love watching them from my living room." She walked over to the large Christmas tree by the picture window facing the lake. She raised her eyebrows. "That tree is huge. How in the world did you get this thing in here?"

Carolina's cheeks turned bright pink. "Thomas brought it over last night." She headed into the kitchen. "Want some coffee?"

Hannah grinned. "No thanks. I've had my limit for the day." She followed her and eased onto the kitchen stool while Carolina fixed herself another cup of coffee.

"So, how is Thomas?" Hannah asked with a suggestive tone in her voice.

"Oh, he's good. Busy with work." Carolina avoided eye contact and instead focused all her attention on stirring the creamer into her hot cup of coffee.

"I wouldn't think there would be a lot of demand for roofers during the winter months." Hannah refused to change the subject.

"Usually there isn't. But with all this snow we are getting lately, people are having issues with their roofs. He's been doing patch jobs and scheduling roofs replacements in spring."

"It's good to know business is doing so well." Hannah bit the inside of her jaw. "I suspect his personal life is doing well. By the looks of things." She glanced over at the tree.

Carolina looked up and blinked like a deer in headlights.

Hannah laughed and placed her hands on the counter. "I don't mean to tease you, Carolina. I think it's great. I hope you and Thomas have the kind of relationship that I did with James. You certainly deserve that kind of love." A slight sting of grief struck her heart.

Carolina's expression softened. She reached out and gently squeezed Hannah's hand. "Thank you for saying that. And I'm sorry that I never had the chance to meet James. Everyone in Hopeton just can't say enough good things about him."

Hannah sighed and nodded. "He was a good man. And I miss him dearly. Sometimes I get so lonely in my house." She glanced over at Phoenix. "I am considering getting a dog."

As if sensing he was part of the conversation, Phoenix looked up from his position curled in front of the fireplace, lifted his leg, and then began licking himself.

Hannah cringed. "Then again. Maybe not."

She shook her head. "Phoenix, stop that." Carolina disciplined. "That dog has no manners."

Hannah laughed. "Well if you are ready to paint, I am ready to start. Are we still painting your bedroom?"

"Yes. And I can't wait. I've chosen Revere Pewter. I'm so tired of this faded yellow. If it looks good, then I'll eventually paint the whole house in that color." Carolina set her cup down and clasped her hands together. "Let's get started."

A few short hours later, they were finished. The trimming-out process took the most time to complete. But once that was done they both rolled on two coats of the pretty paint.

Carolina set the roller back in the nearly empty paint tray and looked around. "I think it looks good."

Hannah nodded. "It does. Good choice of paint." She glanced down at her black garbage bag. "Although I think we might have gotten more paint on ourselves than on the wall."

Carolina looked down and laughed.

After stripping the garbage bag off and tossing it into the garbage can, Hannah washed her hands of any paint residue. Carolina had offered to make lunch for them both, but Hannah had to decline. She had a one o'clock appointment with the director of the hospital in Hopeton. James had made large charitable donations to the hospital over the years and he wanted to talk to her about the loss of her husband and honor him in some way.

His death still felt fresh to her but she knew she'd been putting off meeting with the director for months now.

With Christmas coming up she decided it was time, so she had called him.

As she walked back to her house, bundled up in her winter coat, she wondered how long grief would haunt her. Some days she didn't even feel like getting out of bed. It was one reason she liked being around Carolina so much. If Hannah ever felt like she couldn't make it, she would go over to Carolina's house and see how she fought to make the best of every day.

Hannah stopped at her mailbox and picked up her mail. She rifled through the envelopes on her way up the driveway. She had another pile of Christmas cards from relatives and friends and people who had worked with James. Her heart tugged when she spotted the return address from Alex Banton, her attorney and trustee. Months before he had been diagnosed with cancer, James had set up a trust for her and the children. It was as if he had known his time on earth was limited. She was due for an in-person meeting with Alex to go over some questions she had. She would make a point to call him this week and set something up.

Hannah shoved back her grief-stricken thoughts and put the letter in the back of the pile.

She frowned when she spotted a letter addressed to her with no return address. She quickly unlocked her door and stepped inside the warmth of the house.

She carefully hung up her coat in the closet and stepped out of her boots. She stepped into her slippers, curled up on the couch and turned on the fireplace using the remote.

Skipping over opening the Christmas cards, she instead focused on the letter, carefully lifting the seal. Her eyes scanned the contents of the letter:

"Your husband stole from the company he claimed to love. He wasn't the man everyone thought he was. If you don't want your husband's true character to be revealed then you must make penance for his sins."

Nausea rolled in her stomach and she blinked. The words didn't make sense.

Who would write such a thing? Who would be so cruel? Did James have enemies she didn't know about?

Doubt rolled through her for just a second.

What if the letter was true?

What if she never really knew James like she thought she did?

More importantly, what in the world was she going to do?

CHAPTER 2

*I*t had started snowing again as Hannah drove into Hopeton. She pulled into the parking lot of Mercy Hospital and cut the engine of her Mercedes. She tugged on her gloves and gathered her purse before getting out of her car.

Hannah burrowed down deep in her red-wool coat and hurried to the hospital entrance. Her high-heeled boots made tiny clicking sounds against the concrete as she raced against the falling snow.

Stepping inside the warmth of the hospital, she shook her blonde hair free of snowflakes.

Albert was waiting for her at the elevators. He waved and walked towards her. "Hannah. It's so good to see you. How are you?" He took her hand between his and squeezed.

She gave him a smile. "I'm good, Albert. Trying not to freeze in all this cold weather."

He chuckled. "Missy wanted me to tell you that we

want you to come to dinner at your earliest convenience. She misses you."

A smile formed as she nodded. "Tell her I miss her too. And I'll definitely take her up on her dinner invitation."

He clapped his hands together. "Wonderful. Now let's go into the conference room where we'll be more comfortable."

"Okay." She smiled just as the image of the letter she'd received flashed in her memory.

She forced the ugly image away and reminded herself that whoever had sent the disparaging message had done it as a cruel joke. The accusations weren't true. They couldn't be.

They rode up in the elevator and Hannah tried to mask her angst by making small talk. She asked about his grown kids. His eyes shone with pride as he chatted away about their accomplishments. He, in turn, inquired after her kids, Gregory and Ella.

"It's hard that they're not living in Hopeton. I had hoped they would move closer to home but their jobs are too good and they're happy where they are."

"As long as they are happy, then that's all that matters." He smiled.

She sighed. "True. A parent's job is to prepare them for adulthood. I just wish our little birds didn't fly the nest so soon."

"We are both blessed that we raised such good kids," Albert said wistfully.

"Yes we are." She gave a solid nod.

The elevators opened and they stepped out into a plush area on the top floor. She followed Albert along the carpeted hallway to a large room at the end.

He held the door open. "Come on in."

She stepped inside the large conference room with massive windows providing an amazing view of the small town. A large conference table made of rich mahogany sat in the middle of the room, with buttery-soft-leather chairs surrounding the table. The walls were decorated with abstract art from famous artists across the state of North Carolina. A lone sculpture of a large winged angel sat in the corner, as if overlooking the goings on of the hospital.

He walked over to a table along the wall. "There is coffee and a coffee cake, compliments of Missy."

She melted under his wife's consideration. "She's so kind. I bet it's the lemon cake she made at her ladies' luncheon. It was delicious."

A wide smile broke across his face. "She said you loved it. So, she made it for you today."

"How can I say no to that?" She walked over and took the large slice he'd cut and put on a plate. "Thank you."

She fixed a cup of coffee and brought it, with her cake, over to the table where Albert held out a chair.

Hannah sat and took a sip, sighing softly as the hot coffee slid down her throat, warming her against the weather outside.

Albert took a bite of the lemon-coffee cake and

smiled. "I guess you are wondering why I asked you to come today."

"It is a bit of a mystery."

"As you know James has been such a charitable contributor to our hospital here, as well as the medical research center in Charlotte."

She ran her finger around the rim of the cup. "James cared a lot about making sure the children's wing got the donations it needed."

"He was a good man and dearly missed," Albert's voice was somber.

Hannah felt the same inside, "Some mornings I wake up and forget he's gone," she admitted. "Those days are the worst. But as they say, life goes on." She sighed.

He gave her a sympathetic smile. "Maybe what I have to tell you will lessen the sting of your grief. Hannah, I wanted to be the first to let you know. The board has decided to name the children's wing after James."

"What?" Her eyes widened.

"Yes. And there is going to be a big dedication party on the twenty-third of December."

"Two days before Christmas? But that's less than two weeks away."

"I know. But the board wanted it done before the end of the year and we couldn't think of a better season to celebrate James' generosity than at Christmas."

"That's wonderful. I don't know what to say. What do I need to do?" Her mind raced, forgetting about the letter. "Invitations will have to be sent out. Then there's the caterer as well as a decorator."

He laughed and patted her hand. "Hannah, I didn't mean to tell you all this only to have you worry about the details. Invitations, food, and decorating will all be taken care of. The board is having a professional caterer come in, so you don't have to think about a thing. I promise you, it will be beautiful."

She nodded and relaxed back in the chair.

"The only thing you need to do is make sure you and the kids are there to honor his legacy."

"I can do that." She smiled.

Albert leaned back in his chair. "I don't know if James ever told you, but we were at lunch one time at a Chinese restaurant when a group of soldiers came in. James called the waitress over and told her he was buying their lunch. He told her not to tell the soldiers who paid."

"That sounds like James. He didn't like to be acknowledged when he did something so selfless."

"Imagine his surprise when that group of soldiers all stood up and walked over to our table. The waitress told them he paid for their meal and they wanted to thank him personally. They each shook his hand before they left."

Her mouth gaped. "What did James say?"

"After that everyone in the restaurant came up to him and thanked him. James was so embarrassed that he couldn't get out of there fast enough," Alfred said.

"After that, whenever he paid for someone's meal, he told the waitress when he was leaving."

She smiled. "That sounds exactly like James. He wasn't much for praise."

The rest of the time they spent talking about James and memories they had of him. Hannah lost herself in memories of her late husband. It was bittersweet.

When they were done, Albert escorted her to the entrance of the hospital.

The snow had stopped falling, leaving a fresh blanket of white on the ground. She hurried back to her car thinking how excited she was to tell her kids the wonderful news that their father was going to be honored. They would be so proud. Maybe they would stay long enough and spend Christmas with her at the lake house.

She would have to get a new outfit for the event. Maybe that cute little full-skirted black dress she saw on the Nordstrom website. She had a nice pair of heels sitting in the closet that would work just fine, but this was a huge event. An event that certainly deserved a new pair of sparkly stilettos.

Hannah got into her car feeling completely ecstatic. She started the engine before reaching into her purse for a pen and piece of paper to make a list of things she needed to get done before the big event. She pulled out a sheet of paper and froze.

It was the letter which held the horrible accusations against her husband.

Her stomach clenched as she recalled each horrible word.

She shook her head.

It wasn't true. It was all lies.

It had to be.

Her darling husband James was no monster. He was a man who bought Christmas gifts and set up college funds for a single widowed father of four children. He was the man who bought soldiers a meal before they shipped off overseas. He was kind and generous.

There was no possible way anything in that letter was true.

She forced those intrusive thoughts away and drove back home.

CHAPTER 3

*H*annah had just changed into some comfortable clothes when the doorbell rang.

She slipped on her fur-lined boots, zipped up her designer hoody and headed toward the front door.

"I know you're home, Hannah. Hurry up. It's cold out here."

She rolled her eyes at Bernice's grumbling.

Hannah opened the front door and forced a smile. "Hi Bernice. Come on in."

"Thank you, honey." Bernice came bursting through the door with a small potted Christmas tree. "I can't believe it keeps snowing. And it's not even Christmas, yet."

"I think it's magical. And it looks so pretty especially around the lake." Hannah gazed out the large living room window at the scenic view. The water on the lake was still and looked like glass. The bare trees resembled intricate lace against the gray, overcast sky. The snow blanketed the entire backyard in a puffy white quilt. When her kids were young, they'd be out in the backyard building snowmen and sledding while she made hot chocolate on the stove.

"Earth to Hannah. You haven't heard a word I said." Bernice scowled.

Hannah shook her head. "Sorry. I was just thinking of the past snowfalls we had when the kids were little."

Bernice's expression softened. She patted her hand. "Aww, honey. I know it must be hard this time of year without your James."

Hannah smiled. "It is." Her gaze landed on the little tree.

Bernice brightened. "Well, this should make you feel better. I brought you a little Christmas gift." She placed the tree on the kitchen island.

"It's beautiful, Bernice. Is it from your nursery?" She touched the tiny red and green ornaments on the tiny tree.

"Sure is. Carolina's idea. She said once the harvest items were sold out we needed to prepare for Christmas. I never in my life thought I would be selling anything at Christmas, but since she's been working for me she's given me new ideas and we've been selling poinsettias and these small potted trees. I didn't think anyone would buy one, but when the nursing home found out we had them, they placed an order for all their residents."

"What a nice gesture. Nothing feels like Christmas spirit like a pretty Christmas tree."

"You sound like Carolina." Bernice snorted.

That made Hannah smile. "Sounds like she's good for business."

"I'll admit when I'm wrong. And I was wrong about Carolina. She is one smart cookie when it comes to the nursery business and making things grow." Bernice grinned. "It seems I'm not the only one who was wrong about her. Did she tell you her ex-husband came to see her?"

"No." The smile slid off Hannah's face. "What did he want?"

"I'll let her tell you. It was quite a story." Bernice lifted her eyebrows and nodded knowingly.

Hannah frowned at the older woman. "You can't just leave me hanging like this, Bernice."

"I'm not one for gossip you know." She lifted her chin. "You'll just have to get it from the horse's mouth, so to speak. Well, I've got to be going. I'll see you around." She headed out the front door leaving Hannah standing there with her mouth hanging open.

She glanced at the time. Carolina wouldn't be home from work for another thirty minutes.

That gave her enough time to call her kids and give them the surprise about the hospital dedication.

She went into the kitchen and filled the teakettle with water. She set it on the stove and waited for it to sing. When the water was hot, she turned off the heat and poured the hot water over her favorite bag of green tea.

With a cup of hot tea and her cell phone in hand, she settled on the couch and dialed her daughter, Ella, to share the good news about her father.

CHAPTER 4

*H*annah looked at the time on her watch. Almost six o'clock. Carolina would have been home for at least an hour now. Since learning the news of James' dedication ceremony, she wanted to extend an invitation to her friend.

She wasn't sure what Carolina would like to drink so she got the teakettle ready as well as chilled a bottle of chardonnay. She had made a charcuterie board of cheeses, meats, olives, and nuts. She even put out some doggie treats for Phoenix to nibble on.

The doorbell trilled and she smoothed down her hair before heading to answer it. She flung open the door. Carolina was standing there with bits of snow in her hair and a twinkle in her eye.

"Come in before you freeze to death." Hannah looked behind her. "Phoenix didn't follow you."

"He tried but then he got distracted by a deer near the lake." Carolina walked in and pulled off her coat.

She laid it on the entryway bench before sitting to take her shoes off. "I don't want to track snow into your beautiful house," she said tugging off her boots.

"Oh, I don't worry about things like that. I'm just glad you could come over." Hannah smiled and led the way into the kitchen.

Carolina's eyes softened. "You put out a snack for Phoenix. How thoughtful, Hannah."

"Yes, well, I know he's like family to you. And it's not a bad idea to have your own dog especially when you're walking over here in the dark."

Just then the doorbell rang again. Hannah frowned and picked up her phone to look at her security camera. "I'm not expecting anyone else."

Hannah clicked the camera app on her phone and her mouth dropped. She held out the phone to Carolina. "Would you look at that! Phoenix knows how to ring the doorbell with his nose."

They both watched the camera as the dog pressed his nose to the doorbell. Carolina hurried to the front door and threw it open.

Without asking for an invitation, Phoenix rushed inside and immediately curled up beside the large stone fireplace.

"Phoenix, how did you know how to ring the doorbell?" Carolina put her hands on her hips and smiled at her dog.

"Because he's a smart dog." Hannah grabbed a dog treat off the counter. She walked over to the dog and knelt down.

The dog's head immediately lifted and gently took the dog treat in his mouth. She smiled and patted his head.

"You should post that online. I can send it to you." Hannah walked back into the kitchen.

"I wouldn't know how to post that. I'm not tech savvy." Carolina followed her.

"I didn't know what you wanted to drink so I set out a little bit of everything. I didn't know if you had eaten yet." Hannah waved her hand over the counter laden with food.

"That looks perfect. I had a late lunch so something light is great."

Hannah smiled and handed her a Christmas plate decorated with snowmen and Christmas trees.

"What would you like to drink?" Hannah asked.

Carolina's gaze landed on the bottle of wine. "I'll splurge and have a glass of wine." She smiled.

"We'll fix our plates and sit in the living room by the fireplace." Hannah uncorked the wine and poured them both a glass.

After fixing their plates, they took their food and their wine and sat on the overstuffed couch near the fireplace.

Hannah pointed to the tree on the mantel. "Bernice brought me one of the Christmas trees you guys are selling."

Carolina's mouth dropped open. "That little sneak. I mentioned I was going to bring you one and she beat me to it."

Hannah laughed. "She said you've been a great help with all your ideas. She said she's never been so busy at Christmas."

Carolina snorted. "She told me I ruined her vacation by ordering all the trees and poinsettias. I reminded her that I am perfectly able to run the nursery without her and that she deserves a vacation."

Hannah laughed. "She's not one to let someone help her out."

"No kidding," Carolina took a sip of her wine.

"I have some news to share. I've already called the kids and told them. It's about James."

Carolina set her glass down on a coaster on the coffee table. "What is it?"

Hannah clasped her hands in her lap and looked at her friend. "I met with one of the board members at the hospital and they told me they were dedicating the children's wing to James."

"Oh honey, that's wonderful!" Carolina grasped her friend's hand and then pulled her in for a hug. "When is the ceremony?" Carolina asked.

"December twenty-third."

"Wow, so soon."

"Yes and well, I was wondering if you would come."

"Absolutely! I wouldn't miss it for the world." Carolina's eyes shown with true excitement.

Carolina's friendship was a true treasure. Carolina didn't care if Hannah had ten million dollars or ten dollars. She liked Hannah for herself not what she had, a rarity in people nowadays.

"You'll have to tell me what the dress code is. I've never been to a dedication before."

"You never went with your ex?"

She snorted. "No. He didn't go to things that didn't have a payout for him. Charity was not his strong suit." She popped an olive in her mouth and then grew wide-eyed. "Speaking of my slimy ex, I have an update for you."

Hannah grinned. "I had a feeling you did."

Carolina narrowed her eyes. "Bernice already told you didn't she?"

Hannah shook her head. "All she said was he came to see you. She told me if I wanted to find out anything else I had to ask you."

"Good. It's good to know I can trust Bernice." She frowned. "Kind of."

They both laughed.

"So, tell me. Did he call and say he was coming to visit?" Hannah leaned forward totally intrigued.

Carolina settled back into the couch and took a deep breath. "He had been texting me after Thanksgiving." She grimaced. "It was little things like wishing me a happy holiday. But I never responded. Then he sent a text saying he wanted me to call him. I didn't. I called my lawyer instead. I figured he was trying to wiggle his way out of paying alimony. My attorney said if he had something to say he could convey it through my attorney."

Hannah nodded. "I agree."

"Anyway, I had forgotten about it until a few days

ago. I got a knock at the door. Phoenix was barking his head off, which he doesn't normally do. I open the door and Chris is standing there."

Hannah felt her eyes widen.

"The first thing out of my mouth was 'what are you doing here?' He looked at me and blinked. When he finally spoke, he told me I looked beautiful." Carolina rolled her eyes.

"He said I had lost weight, which I had, thanks to the stress of the divorce."

"What a jerk," Hannah sneered.

"No kidding. I asked again what he was doing there. He said he needed to talk to me. I told him that wasn't a good idea and that he needed to call my attorney. He begged me for just one minute of my time." Carolina stopped and took a sip of her wine. "Chris Johnson has never begged me for anything in his life."

"Were you nervous? I mean this was the first time you saw him since the divorce, right?"

"Right." She frowned. "I wasn't really nervous. Just put out. I had plans that night. Thomas was picking me up for dinner. I finally told him this conversation had to be quick. So I let him in."

Hannah sat on the edge of her seat waiting to hear more.

"He came in and I could see he was surprised to see how much work I had done on the lake house." Carolina arched a brow. "I told him there was a lot to do to get it back in livable shape. The man didn't even have the common courtesy to look ashamed that he'd let the lake house get run down." She shook her head.

"I have to ask. When you saw him, did you have any feelings toward him?"

Carolina frowned and looked thoughtful for a moment. "Honestly? Not like I thought I would. He looked different to me. He wasn't the same dashing man I always thought him to be. When I first met him, I thought he was the smartest and most handsome man I had ever laid eyes on. Now, although he looked the same, he wasn't appealing. It was almost like his mask had slid off and I was seeing what was underneath." She frowned and looked at Hannah. "That sounds weird doesn't it?"

"No. It actually sounds refreshingly…honest." She waved her hand. "So what did he want?"

Carolina grinned. "He admitted he made a horrible mistake with Kylie. He said he was sorry and he wanted me to come back."

Hannah's jaw dropped.

"I had the same reaction!" Carolina laughed.

Hannah took an olive from the tray. "What did you say?"

"I was stunned. Chris has never said the word, sorry, in his life. I didn't know what to say. I just let him ramble." Carolina shook her head. "He said that Kylie doesn't cook at all. The most she's made since they've been married is chicken nuggets. He said the house is a mess on the days the maid doesn't come and Kylie doesn't work in the flower beds. He said she spends all her time on the couch complaining her back hurts and shops online using his credit card."

Hannah grinned. "Sounds like karma is catching up to him."

"I know, right?" Carolina smirked. "I told him that we were divorced and never getting back together. I told him he was going to be a father in a few months so he better make things right with Kylie. He said he didn't care. He said he didn't even think the baby was his."

"Oh my gosh!" Hannah put her hand over her mouth. "What do you think? Is the baby his?"

"Honestly? I think it's his. He's just trying to get out of the mess he's made. I told him he needed to leave because I had plans. He grabbed my hands, said he was sorry and he'd make it up to me if I just came back. That's when Thomas walked in."

Hannah grinned. "This is just like a movie."

"I know, but better." Carolina took another sip before she continued. "Thomas sees me pushing Chris off of me and comes barreling toward us. He grabs Chris by the neck and tossed him on the couch. He said if he ever sees him lay a hand on me again he'll beat him to a pulp."

"Chris was so stunned when Thomas appeared out of nowhere, that he scrambled to his feet and ran out the door with Phoenix nipping at his heels."

Hannah looked over at the sleeping dog. "Good dog."

"I explained to Thomas who Chris was and why he

was there. I made it clear that I was never getting back together with Chris. We went on to dinner and he even took me dancing." Carolina beamed. "I can't tell you the last time I went dancing."

"That's wonderful, Carolina. I'm glad you finally found a man who will treat you right. Thomas is a good man."

"Thank you. Since you have experience being married to a good man I really appreciate that."

Hannah's smile faltered.

Carolina frowned. "Is everything okay?"

"Yes, of course. I'm just wondering something."

"Wondering what?"

"When you married Chris, did you have any inkling to his true character?"

Carolina burst out laughing. "Are you kidding? Honey, I had no self-esteem when I met him. I thought I was lucky just to get him to look at me twice." She shook her head. "I was always so afraid that he was going to wake up one day and realize he made a mistake. And then it happened."

"Oh Carolina." Hannah reached out and squeezed her friend's hands.

"But that's all in the past. I'm happier now and more independent than I have ever been."

"You deserve all the happiness in the world." Hannah meant every word.

"If I can have half the happiness that you and James had, then that will be more than enough for me."

Hannah cleared her throat. "Well, no one really knows anyone until after they're married, right?"

Carolina shook her head. "You knew your husband. I mean you guys had a wonderful marriage and everyone in Hopeton always raves about what a wonderful man he was. So generous and giving."

Hannah smiled and looked away.

"Oh honey. I'm sorry. I didn't mean to upset you. I know you must miss him terribly during the holidays." Carolina reached for her hand.

"I do," Hannah said softly. She didn't want her friend to know about the letter she'd gotten. Not now.

She had to do a little investigation of her own before telling a soul about what had been said about James.

Right now, she just needed to keep his reputation in good standing. For as long as it took.

CHAPTER 5

*H*annah was thankful that today it had not snowed and the roads were good enough to drive. She had a lot to get done. Besides preparing for Christmas, she had to get ready for James' dedication ceremony. She'd called her trustee's office to talk to him about the trust, but his secretary had said he was skiing in Aspen with his family. So she'd called her son, Gregory instead to ask if he'd noticed any irregularities regarding the trust. He'd been rushing to get to a meeting with a new client in Charlotte who wanted Gregory to design a state-of-the-art smart home. The client was a recent transplant from Seattle and had made his millions in real estate.

Hannah knew her son and didn't go into any details over the phone. He was driven when it came to work, just like his father, so she wished him good luck and told him to call her later.

So she decided to focus on her to-do list.

Hannah dropped off some presents at her church for the annual Christmas toy drive for low-income families.

She looked forward to shopping for the kids since hers were grown. She spent hours on the internet searching for the most popular toys of the season, then spared no expense and splurged.

After delivering the toys, Hannah talked to the church secretary for a while before she headed off to her next destination, to find a dress for the ceremony.

She took the long way and turned down the street where her husband's business was located.

She slowed as the building came into view. He had grown Stars Global, the technology company, from the ground up. He'd brought on his best friend, Fred Sinclair, as his partner. With lots of hard work and lots of hours, they'd doubled the business within the first two years. A businessman from New York had approached James to buy the business. He offered him two million dollars. James had declined. He told Hannah the business would be worth twice that much within a year. He'd been wrong.

Within a year, Stars Global, had accelerated to a worth of over six million. Every year after that, it continued to grow.

The business had become a relatively tight-knit company with surprising wealth in the small town of Hopeton.

James always had a golden touch when it came to making money. In their early years of marriage, he had bought and flipped properties and earned money. After starting the business, the only properties he bought were vacation properties, destinations where James wanted to spend time. At one time they had houses in Hawaii, Montana, and Florida.

Once the kids were grown, they'd sold the houses in Florida and Hawaii, and held onto the house in Montana for when they wanted to go skiing.

Changing her mind about going dress shopping, she turned into the parking lot of the building. There were fewer cars and she figured it was because of some people taking off for the holidays.

Hannah turned the car off and glanced over at the seat on the passenger's side. She'd stopped by the drugstore when she left the house and picked up some gift cards for her out-of-town relatives. Now that she was here, she decided to put the gift cards to better use. She grabbed them and stuck them in her purse before she hurried out of the car.

Hannah tugged the door and spotted Terri Hoggard, the receptionist, on the phone. Terri spotted Hannah and blinked twice, clearly surprised to see her.

Terri quickly finished the call and stood up and giggled. "Hannah. I didn't know you were dropping by. Come on back. Let me unlock the door." She unlocked the door leading back to the hallway of offices. Terri wore a short black skirt and red blouse that showed off her curves. She smiled widely and held out her arms. Hannah hugged her.

"It's so good to see you. You're still as beautiful as ever." Terri smiled and laughed.

"You're sweet. You look great, too." Hannah always thought Terri had a bit of a crush on her husband. But James had vehemently denied it was true. While she went out of her way to be nice, he found her too silly, laughing at every little thing. In fact he said she was carrying a torch for Fred.

"What are you doing here? Did you have an appointment to meet with Mark that I forgot about?" She laughed again. "I hope I didn't miss something on the schedule."

"No, no. I just wanted to drop by and give everyone a gift card and wish them Merry Christmas." She pulled out the cards from her purse.

"Well, aren't you the sweetest!" Terri cackled and clasped her hands together. "Come on back and I'll let you say hi to everyone." She walked with Hannah to the first door which was Mike Hanover's office. Mike had been with the company from the start. When James had gotten sick, he had asked Mike to take over because he trusted him so much.

Hannah wondered if her husband regretted his best friend Fred leaving the company. She knew in her heart that if he had stayed he would have been put in charge instead of Mike.

"Come in." Mike's deep voice called out.

Terri opened the door and popped her head in. "Look who dropped by." She stepped aside so he could see Hannah.

"Hannah! Isn't this a welcome surprise?" He stood and walked around the desk. He enveloped her small frame in his arms.

"Hi, Mike. How are you?" She pulled back and looked up into his face.

"I'm doing better than I deserve." He smiled down at her.

"I was in the neighborhood and I wanted to drop by to wish everyone a Merry Christmas." She opened her purse and pulled out the gift cards. "And I have some goodies to hand out."

"How thoughtful of you." He waved his hand at the chair. "Here, sit."

"Hannah, would you like some coffee or something to drink?" Terri asked. "I ordered this special tea from Africa that has special antioxidants."

"No, thank you, Terri."

"Oh, well, I'll be at the desk if either of you need anything." Terri smiled and shut the door behind her leaving them their privacy.

"Are you ready for Christmas?" Mike leaned back in his chair. "Seems like it comes earlier every year."

"I know. Ella, Gregory, and Gregory's wife, Shelia are coming in, so that's good." Her smile faltered. "How is Emily doing?"

He sighed. "She's doing good. We had to move her mom in with us. Her dementia has gotten worse and Emily can't seem to bring herself to put her in a nursing home."

Hannah gave him a sympathetic smile. "That has to be hard."

"Emily's wearing herself out. I'd like to hire some extra help, but her insurance won't pay for it." He ran his hands through his hair.

"I had no idea. What about hiring someone to come in and help?"

"I looked into it, but it's expensive and with business down right now, I just can't make it work."

Her gut tightened. "Business is down?"

"Yeah. I'm sure it's just the holidays. It's bound to pick up."

He must have seen the distressed look on her face because he reached over and patted her hand. "It's nothing for you to worry about."

Part of her wanted to get up and leave that instant. She had always heard that ignorance is bliss. Maybe she should just ignore the letter and stay in her ignorant blissful state of how things were without stirring the past up.

But deep down she knew she couldn't.

"Mike, can I ask you something?"

"Sure." He steepled his fingers under his chin and gave her his full attention.

"The business... is the business not doing well?"

A faint look of worry crossed his eyes, but he quickly covered with a smile. "Hannah, you know James built a good business and we're not going to let it go down the drain. Things just slow right now. Some of our clients are looking at getting their software overseas because it's cheaper. But it's not good quality. They'll see that. That's all. Nothing for you to worry about."

She relaxed a little. "You'd tell me if there was a problem, right?"

He smile and nodded. "Yes, Hannah. I know how much the business meant to James and to you." His desk phone rang and he grew serious when he saw who was calling. "I'm sorry, Hannah. I really need to take this."

"Of course." She stood and smiled. "I'll just drop these off to the employees."

"They'll be glad to see you." He smiled and then picked up the phone.

Hannah quietly shut the door behind her. From the hallway, she could still hear Terri on the phone laughing and talking. She headed down the hallway to the next door and knocked.

"Come in." Jonas Still called out.

She opened the door and peered in. "Hi, Jonas."

"Hannah." He jumped up from behind his desk and came around to greet her. "I didn't expect you." He pulled her into a hug.

When she pulled away, she smiled. "I made an unannounced trip. Just wanted to see everyone before the holidays."

"It's so good to see you. This place is certainly not the same without James." He gave her a small smile.

"He loved this business and the people who worked here. You all meant a lot to him." She patted his hand.

"And I wanted to drop these by to everyone." She pulled out a gift card and handed it to him. "Merry Christmas, Jonas."

"How generous of you." He took the gift and gave her a grateful smile. "How are you doing?"

"I'm surviving." She nodded. The grief never went away, but the edges weren't as hard against her heart as they once were.

"I don't want to keep you from work. I just wanted to wish you a Merry Christmas."

"Merry Christmas, Hannah." He gave her another hug.

She went from office to office, handing out the gift cards and visiting briefly with James' former coworkers. When he started the business, he made an effort to treat everyone like family and it had resonated within their work. After being diagnosed with cancer, he'd told them he would be back at work in no time after his chemo.

But the cancer had been so far advanced that James had never come back to work.

Hannah gave Terri another hug before heading out to her car.

She sat outside, her hands gripping the steering wheel, staring at the business her husband had built.

The letter couldn't be true. It was a cruel joke.

Besides if he had stolen money from the business, he would have been caught.

She would have known.

Her phone buzzed with a text message pulling her out of her own thoughts.

She reached for the phone.

"Don't forget to bring your famous dip for our gathering tonight." ~Elena

Hannah sighed as she sent a confirmation text.

She'd been meeting with Elena and her other friends as long as she could remember. Their kids had grown up together and sometimes they'd even taken vacations together.

But after James had died she had pulled back from meeting with the ladies. She found she preferred the company of Carolina and her garbage bag shirt, to Elena and her latest diamond bracelet that her husband had brought her from his last business trip in New York.

She had changed.

She supposed it was possible for people to change.

Hannah leaned back against the seat of the car. She'd seen movies where wives learned their husbands were not who they had thought. She'd always insisted that would never be her. James was too genuine, thoughtful, and generous. He was nothing like those husbands.

Of course, that's the same thing those wives thought. They believed their husbands were incapable of deception.

The notion shook her to the core. With slightly trembling hands, she started the car and drove back to her house.

CHAPTER 6

"*H*annah, you must give me the recipe for this crab dip. It's simply divine." Elena Sakul popped another pita chip loaded with crab dip into her mouth.

"It's really simple, actually." Hannah chuckled. "It's cream cheese…"

Elena waved her hand in the air and shook her head. "Don't even bother telling me. You must write it down. The older I get the worse my memory gets. Why, this morning I went outside and then just stood there on my front porch. I knew I had gone out for something but couldn't remember what it was for."

Hannah frowned. "Did it come to you?"

"Yes, thirty minutes later when I heard my dog, Lawrence, yelping at the front door." She shook her head. "I let the poor thing out and forgot about him. He had icicles hanging off his eyebrows."

Hannah snickered. Elena's Yorkie may be little, but

he was an ankle biter and tried to bite everyone that entered her house. He'd even drawn blood on Betty's leg once.

Betty narrowed her eyes. "A little cold won't hurt Lawrence."

"Yes, well, I'll be sure to write down the recipe for the dip." Hannah stifled a grin and pulled a pen out of her purse. "Do you have some paper?"

"Yes, dear. In the top drawer of the kitchen island." Elena stuffed another chip in her mouth.

Hannah resisted the urge to roll her eyes and stood. She made her way to the kitchen admiring the new wall color.

Elena was notorious for painting and redecorating her entire house every time she caught whiff of what the hot new decorating themes were going to be for the year.

She usually ended up with more misses than hits when it came to design.

But this wall color was one of the hits.

"What's the name of this paint color?" Hannah called out as she dug through the junk drawer in the kitchen.

"It's Accessible Beige. Looks good in every light." Elena said.

Hannah nodded. She made a mental note to see if it would look good in her bedroom.

She found a notepad and pulled it out. She began writing the recipe down on the paper.

"Can you believe she painted again?" Betty

muttered as she walked over to the refrigerator. She filled her glass with water.

"I'm liking this color. I may use it myself." Hannah ripped off the sheet and put the notepad back in the drawer.

Betty moved closer. "Did you hear about Richard?" She murmured.

Hannah frowned. "Elena's Richard? No."

"Looks like he's not the doting husband Elena wants us to believe." Betty whispered. "Rumor has it he's got a mistress in a penthouse in New York."

Hannah lifted her chin. "Betty, you know better than to give an ear to idle gossip."

"It's not gossip. It's the truth." Betty crossed her arms and arched her brow. "I know it's the truth because my daughter Lindsey saw them when she was on her girls' trip to New York. They were cozied up in a booth at some swanky restaurant. When they got up to leave my daughter followed them back to the penthouse." She paused for effect. "At a distance, of course."

Hannah arched her brow. "So Lindsey actually went into the penthouse?"

Betty lifted her chin, perturbed at being questioned. "No. She flirted with the doorman until he disclosed that Richard was living with his girlfriend there. Said the woman couldn't be over twenty-five."

Hannah's stomach tightened. She hated drama. She hated gossip even worse.

"Does Elena know?" Hannah whispered while glancing around to make sure no one overheard.

"I haven't said anything. But the way she carries on about her dear Richard, I'm guessing not. Or maybe she does know and prefers to live with her eyes closed."

Hannah shook her head, stunned. "I can't believe it."

"Can't believe what dear?" Elena walked in.

Betty straightened and gave Elena a sad expression. "Hannah just can't believe James is gone. It's her first Christmas without him, you know." She looked at Hannah and patted her arm.

Elena's face shifted into a sympathetic mask. "Oh dear. I just can't imagine what you are going through. I mean, you and James were so perfect and so happy. It's the same with me and Richard. I can't imagine a life without him." She hugged Hannah, squeezing her tight like she was trying to pour strength into her weary soul.

Hannah's gut tightened with guilt. Betty avoided her gaze.

Elena pulled back and looked at her with a smile. "Don't worry dear. James is still with you, in here." She tapped Hannah on her chest above her heart.

Hannah smiled. "Thank you, Elena." She cleared her throat. "Enough with this melancholy mood. We should be focusing on the blessings in our lives."

"Yes. I'll drink to that." Betty took a big drink of her water and headed back to the other women in the dining room.

"Come dear. I'll show you what Richard brought me back from New York this last trip. He must have missed me terribly to buy me not one, but two gifts."

Hannah kept her mouth shut as Elena showed off her husband's gifts.

But in the back of her mind, a tiny small voice kept asking if she had really ever known James.

Were she and Elena the same when it came to husbands?

CHAPTER 7

*H*annah had forgotten to get her mail out of the mailbox the day before, so she was busy concentrating on cradling the large amount of mail in her arms while trying not to slip on the icy patches in her driveway. When James was alive, he paid a service to come out and take care of clearing the driveway so she wouldn't slip.

It was odd to her that the little things that James did to make her life easier, were now the things that reminded her of him.

Luckily, she made it back to the front door without dropping any of the mail or slipping.

Hannah stepped inside and piled the mail on the foyer table before she shoved out of her winter coat. She pulled off her boots and placed them in the plastic boot tray by the door, and then slipped on her fuzzy house shoes.

Hannah carried her mail into the living room and

grabbed her letter opener before she curled up on the couch.

Hannah smiled as she read a Christmas card from Carolina. Her neighbor had written a thoughtful note inside and it made Hannah really cherish their friendship.

She had ten more Christmas cards from family and friends located across the states. She reached for the water bill when she spotted a letter without a return address.

She scowled as her fingers brushed over the slightly familiar handwriting. A sense of dread washed over her.

Hannah picked up the letter, slid the letter opener along the seal, and carefully opened it.

"If you don't want your precious children to know what their father really did, you need to pay up."

Fear made her blood turn to ice.

She swallowed hard.

"Now they are threatening my children?" For just a second she considered going to the cops. They could help her.

But what if it was true? Had James stolen money from the company he claimed to love?

He'd given her the house of her dreams, vacations everywhere she wanted to go, had nice trust funds set up for both children, and left her a wealthy woman. Her inheritance would keep her comfortable for the rest of her days as well as the trust he established for her portion of the business.

She was there by his side all those years…through all the ups and downs of building a successful business. She'd watched him toil, waking in the early hours before dawn and often not coming to bed until after midnight. While he always carved time for the family, he certainly didn't skimp on what it took to run Stars Global. He felt immense financial responsibility, not only for their family, but for the employees and their families. Much was at stake if it failed, and she knew how much that responsibility weighed on her husband. Yet, he'd pulled it off beautifully. Few knew the sacrifices he made to get there.

Had building his fortune come at a price?

Hannah's gaze lingered on Carolina's Christmas card. She longed to confide in her friend.

But before she could do that, she needed to dig for some more concrete evidence for herself before she spoke to her friend and marred her dead husband's reputation.

She leaned her head back against the couch and closed her eyes, racking her brain as to how to go about finding out more information.

Hannah bolted up as an idea formed in her brain.

Fred Sinclair. James' trusted best friend and former partner.

If James had embezzled money from the company, Fred would know.

She grabbed her phone and went through her contact list. Within seconds she found Fred's number.

She quickly dialed the number and waited.

The call quickly went to voice mail.

She sighed and pressed end without leaving a message.

After Fred left the company, he sold his home in Hopeton. She'd heard that he had moved away but wasn't sure where.

If anyone still had an address for him, Terri, the secretary from Stars Global, would have it on file.

She made a quick call and Terri said she would look for his last forwarding address and send it via text.

Hannah couldn't sit still. She needed something to occupy her mind and hands until Terri called her back.

She knew just the thing to keep her hands and mind occupied while she waited.

Hannah busied herself with pulling out the Christmas decorations. The tree had been done and the mantel was the last area to be decorated.

She fluffed the greenery and carefully arranged it until it filled in the empty spaces. She pulled out some brilliant red sparkly ribbon and began working it through the greenery. She worked with the ribbon until she was satisfied with the appearance.

Then she placed some vintage ornaments she'd found on vacation one year throughout the mantel , filling in the bare spots.

Hannah stood back and assessed her skills.

The doorbell rang, echoing through the house.

She moved the empty plastic container out of the way and made her way to the door.

Hannah opened it to find Carolina standing there with Phoenix at her side.

"Carolina, I wasn't expecting you." She moved out of the doorway. "Please come in."

Carolina grinned and stepped inside. Phoenix raced past her to his spot in front of the fireplace.

"Phoenix, you haven't been asked." Carolina pulled off her coat and set it on the entryway bench.

"It's fine. He's welcome any time." She waited until Carolina pulled off her boots and walked her into the living room. "Would you like something to drink? I have a new cinnamon tea that just came in."

"That sounds delightful." Carolina stood by the fireplace and held her hands out to the blazing fire. "Your mantel is gorgeous. Did the same decorator who did your tree do it as well?"

Hannah smiled as she fixed them both hot cups of tea. "No. I did the mantel. I figured I needed to get it done before I got too busy with the holidays."

"I wish I had a decorator's eye like you." Carolina smiled and took the hot cup of tea that Hannah handed her and took a sip.

Hannah smiled. "That's very kind of you to say. And any time you want some help with your lake house let me know. I'll be more than happy to help."

Carolina smiled and set the cup down on a coaster. "I'm happy to hear that. That's why I'm here. I have some paint colors and I can't decide what to choose. I'd like to get this done before Christmas." She pulled some paint swatches out of her purse.

Hannah grinned and took the swatches. She walked over to the wall and held them up.

"They are so similar that I can't tell what the difference is." Carolina sighed and sat down. "But I'm scared to pick one because it might be the wrong color."

"Never be afraid of choosing the wrong color. If you do, then just paint over it."

"I'm afraid I'm still pinching pennies. I budgeted enough this month for one chance at getting it right." Carolina smiled.

Hannah moved to a different wall and held up the samples. "Look, you can tell that this color changes in the light. This one stays the same. When choosing a color always move the sample around the house so different lights hit it."

Carolina walked over and studied the samples. "That's pretty smart." She pointed to the greige color and nodded. "That's the color I want."

"I agree." Hannah handed her samples back to her. "Can you stay a minute, or do you have to rush back?"

"I'm off today so I have the whole day to myself." Carolina settled back on the couch.

"Nice. I'm glad Bernice isn't working you to death."

"Me, too." Carolina sighed. "But she is giving me more and more control at the nursery. That's actually surprising."

"Wow. You must be making a wonderful impression on her." Hannah nodded.

"I think she's just wanting to take more vacations. I

overheard her on a Zoom call talking to some guy she met online."

Hannah froze. "Bernice met a guy?"

"I know! I was as surprised as you." Carolina laughed. "She's always putting men down, but I think deep down she's lonely."

Hannah nodded. "You're probably right."

Carolina smiled. "I'm taking the opportunity to order some new plants for spring. She's always ordered petunias in all shades of colors. This year I'm adding daffodils, tulips, and crocuses."

"How wonderful. I'll be sure to get my order in soon." Hannah sighed. "My flowerbeds really need to be redone."

"Well, I can certainly help with that. Just let me know what you want and I can put some ideas together."

"Thank you, Carolina. You're a good friend."

"So are you. I'm lucky I found you when I moved to Hopeton. Lord knows, I needed to find some real friends." She sighed and shook her head.

"Carolina, can I ask you a question?" Hannah leaned forward. "It's kind of personal. Well, very personal."

"Sure. You can ask me anything. I'm an open book." Carolina blinked as if surprising herself. "You know I wasn't always like that. I was always pretending to be something I wasn't. Just to try to fit in." She straightened. "You know, it feels good to realize that."

"I bet." Hannah took a deep breath and blew it out, readying herself. "When you were married, did your ex-husband ever act in a way that would make you suspicious?"

Carolina frowned and thought for a second. "You know. Looking back now, I do. But when I was in the relationship, I couldn't see any red flags."

Hannah cocked her head. "Red flags, like what?"

Carolina took a sip. "Well, during the last year of our marriage he was never home early. He always came in late. Even on our anniversary." She narrowed her eyes. "He always took me out to eat on our anniversary. Always to a nice restaurant. Except for the last anniversary. He insisted that I cook a nice dinner and we eat it at home. He said he missed us eating together. I thought it was sweet, but now I know he didn't want his mistress to see us together." She shook her head. "Plus, she doesn't cook, so he was probably starving for a homecooked meal. The idiot."

Hannah cracked a smile. "That must have been really hard for you. Going through a divorce."

"It was." Carolina sighed and faced Hannah. "Can I be honest?"

"Of course."

"The betrayal and heartbreak were tough enough. But having people realize your marriage was a lie, was a bitter pill to swallow. I have to admit, having to face people's criticism and gossip was worse." She shook her head. "Isn't that crazy? That I cared so much what others thought?"

"It seems pretty normal to me." Hannah's words came out muttered. She studied the mug of tea.

Carolina rested her hand on Hannah's arm. "Look at me. I've upset you. I didn't mean to. The holidays are supposed to be full of peace and joy."

Hannah squeezed her friend's hand. "I promise, you haven't upset me. If anything you always manage to cheer me up. To make me feel like everything will be okay."

Carolina smiled. "That's because it will be. Besides, you didn't have a marriage like mine. Your marriage was built on love and honesty."

After Carolina and Phoenix left, Hannah stood at the window overlooking the lake. Her friend's words rolled around in her head.

Love and honesty.

Had her marriage been built on that? Or had she, like Carolina been deceived?

Her phone rang and she picked it up. "Hello?"

"Hannah, it's Terri. I have Fred's last address. It's in Charleston, South Carolina. I'll text you the address. But I don't know if he still lives there."

"Thank you, Terri. I appreciate it."

"If you get in touch with him, let me know. I need a current contact for our records."

"Will do, Terri. Thanks again." Hannah ended the call.

She was determined now, more than ever to discover whether her marriage foundation had been built on rock. . . or sand.

CHAPTER 8

Hannah drove slowly down the narrow streets of Charleston. She wished she had confided in Carolina so she could have come along with her.

She glanced down at the navigation system and bit her lip. She was a block away from where Fred lived.

She turned down the street and drove two blocks before the navigation was telling her she had arrived at her destination.

Hannah stopped in front of the house and tried to figure out where to park.

The historical home had a gated entrance off the street where the owner could park. Other than parking on the street, she was out of options.

Hannah backed up and parked as close to the curb as she dared, then she gathered her purse and got out of the car.

"Good morning." An older gentleman tipped his hat as he walked past with a little dog on a pink leash.

"Good morning," she smiled and snuggled down into her coat. She glanced at the address that Terri had sent and compared it to what was on the house. It was definitely the right house.

Taking a deep breath, she rang the doorbell.

It took a few minutes but she finally heard footsteps on the other side of the door.

She braced herself for seeing Fred for the first time since he'd left the business.

The door swung open and a blonde-haired woman stood there wearing white pants, a brown sweater, and tall brown boots. She wore a double-strand-pearl necklace and matching earrings. Her short blonde hair was stylishly cut and Hannah recognized the designer scarf around her neck as Hermes.

"Can I help you?" the stranger smiled.

"I hope so." Hannah remembered her manners and forced a smile. "My name is Hannah Reece and I'm looking for Fred Sinclair. He and my husband used to own a business together and I was told he lived here. I tried calling the number but it said it was no longer in service."

"I'm Nancy Huntsman. My husband and I bought the house from Fred a little over a year ago. I think he left a forwarding address. Come in and let me see if I can find it." She stepped back so Hannah could enter.

"Thank you so much." Hannah stepped inside

feeling more than a little disappointed that she'd run into a dead end.

"Come on into the kitchen. I think I might have his information in the junk drawer."

Hannah followed Nancy deeper into the house, taking the opportunity to appreciate the historical architecture.

Nancy stopped at the coffee maker. "I was just about to make another cup for myself. Would you care for one?"

"Thank you, I would. It's terribly cold out today." She glanced out the window. Despite the brilliant sun the wind had chilled her to the bone.

Nancy nodded. "I moved to Charleston to get away from the winter weather. Dickie, my husband says he's going to buy a condo in Miami so we can stay down there during the cold months." She busied herself making two cups of coffee.

"I'm from North Carolina, so I'm used to the cold. But you're right. I don't remember Charleston being this cold in previous years. Where did you moved from, if you don't mind me asking?"

Nancy handed her a cup of coffee and set the cream and sugar in front of her on the kitchen island.

Nancy took a sip of coffee. "We're originally from Vermont. We moved here to escape the snow."

"I've never been to Vermont but always wanted to go. I think it comes from watching *White Christmas* too many times."

Nancy chuckled. "I've heard so many Southerners

say that. Snow is pretty to look at, but not nice when you have to drive on the interstate to get to work."

Hannah nodded. "We Southerners tend to romanticize things a bit."

Nancy grinned. "Charleston is certainly a romantic city. We visited Charleston on vacation and fell in love with the city and its people. Charlestonians enjoy a slower pace of life and people tend to care about one another. Within the first two days of moving in I had neighbors up and down the street bringing me a dessert or a casserole. Not to mention offers of visiting their churches."

"That sounds about right." Hannah laughed. "And we do love a good casserole. I make a really good corn casserole for Thanksgiving," Hannah admitted.

"My poor Dickie has to take me out every night. But he knew when he married me that I couldn't cook nor had any inclination to learn. He knew what he was getting himself into." Nancy shook her head. "Your husband's a lucky man. I bet you keep him well fed."

"My husband's…gone." Hannah swallowed hard. "He died of cancer."

Nancy's eyes grew wide and her hand flew to her mouth. "Oh, I'm so sorry. I shouldn't have said anything," her gaze drifted to Hannah's right hand.

Hannah touched her wedding ring. "I guess I should take it off but I'm not ready. Not yet. Besides just because he died doesn't mean we stopped being married." She looked down. "I guess that's a very weird way to look at things."

Nancy reached over and gave her hand a squeeze. "I think it's lovely. A lot of people move on too fast. I can tell he meant a lot to you."

Hannah nodded. "He did."

Uneasy silence stretched between them and Nancy busied herself searching through her junk drawer.

She finally pulled out a scrap of paper and studied it.

She held it out to Hannah. "It's the last address that his realtor gave us. Looks like he moved back to North Carolina. We had a lot of his mail coming to us at first but nothing these last few months."

Hannah took it. "He moved back to Charlotte. That's not far from Hopeton." She looked up. "I'm surprised he didn't tell anyone he was back in North Carolina."

"I don't know. Maybe he was afraid of people finding out he had to sell and move back."

Hannah frowned. "Had to sell?"

Nancy gave her a strained look. "Well, yes. The house was going to go into foreclosure because of missed payments. So he did a short sale. We got the house for less than what he paid for it."

Hannah cocked her head. "Really? That surprises me. When he left the company he had a large compensation package."

"Well, you never know what goes on in people's lives."

Hannah nodded. "Truer words have never been spoken."

CHAPTER 9

*A*fter thanking Nancy for the coffee and Fred's address, Hannah drove to some local shops to see if she could find something suitable for James' dedication ceremony.

She tried on different dresses until she found one in red that looked perfect on her. She even splurged and bought new heels.

She wished she had brought Carolina with her so she could enjoy Charleston as well.

Maybe they could set up a girl's trip after the holidays. They could get an Airbnb on the beach for a long weekend. Maybe they could find a house that allowed pets and even take Phoenix.

As she drove over the Arthur Ravenel Bridge she thought of the many times James had flown her down here to have dinner at 82 Queen.

She smiled at the sweet memories. James was like

that. A man who kept her on her toes with surprise trips and gestures.

Her smile faltered.

Maybe he had been able to afford that lifestyle because he'd actually done what he'd been accused of in the letter.

Had he embezzled money from the company?

Her hands tightened on the steering wheel. The drive home was too lonely with only her suspicions and doubts in her head to keep her company.

She passed a billboard along the highway once she crossed into North Carolina. It was an advertisement for a criminal defense attorney touting justice for victims of fraud and embezzlement.

She swallowed hard. She'd been so focused on clearing her husband's name, she'd not thought about the legal ramifications for the victims of embezzlement.

Could she be held liable? Could she be prosecuted? Could her children? Could she face jail time?

When she finally pulled into her garage late that night, she was exhausted from the mental mind games she'd put herself through.

She had only stopped to get gas and had forgone dinner.

She couldn't stomach anything right now.

She climbed out of her car and gathered her items.

Once inside, she put away her new dress and turned on the water in her large tub.

She wanted nothing more than to soak in a fragrant bubble bath and then climb into bed.

By the time her head hit the pillow, she was asleep.

CHAPTER 10

*H*annah was doctoring her second cup of coffee with cream and sugar when her cell phone rang. She picked it up and frowned when she saw a text message from an unknown number.

"You have until December 22 to get one million dollars together to send to a secure bank account. If you go to the police or tell anyone, I'll make sure everyone in the state of North Carolina knows that your husband stole money from the company he claimed to love. His reputation, and yours, will be ruined. Not to mention the legal ramifications you will suffer."

Hannah dropped the phone on the hardwood floor. Now they had her phone number.

Fear welled up inside of her until she was choking on it.

Her knees crumbled and she fell to the floor. She scrambled to the phone and sent a quick reply.

"Who is this?"

"In case you are wondering, this phone can't be tracked. You'll get a text on December 22 with the account information. If you are late depositing the money, then your husband's mishandling of his company's funds will be reported all over the news."

Hannah typed in with trembling hands. "Why are you doing this?"

She watched for a reply but none was sent.

Confusion washed over her. Why was this happening?

She couldn't just sit here and do nothing.

She needed answers, no matter how hard it was to face the truth.

Hannah scrambled to her feet and hurried to her husband's office.

Her hand froze on the door handle.

She'd not been inside this room since his death. She couldn't bring herself to step into the room and be reminded that all she had left of him were memories.

Hannah took a steadying breath and turned the doorknob.

Hannah stepped inside and inhaled deeply. James' cologne of sandalwood and cedar still hung heavy in the air.

She'd bought him that cologne three Christmases ago, and he liked it so much that she continued to gift it to him for Father's Day as well.

She glanced around the room at the large library of books that lined the dark walls. When he built the house, he made sure to include a huge library in the office because of Hannah's love of books. He even included a rolling ladder so she could reach the top shelves.

Hannah walked over to his desk and sunk into his leather chair.

The desk faced the window overlooking the lake. The water was like glass against the banks of glistening snow. She often wondered how he could get any work done with such a beautiful view.

She turned on the computer and glanced around the pristine desk.

James was nothing if not a perfectionist. He made it a habit to clear off his desk every night. He said a clean desk helped him start the day off right.

He did the same with his desk at work.

She clicked on different files in his digital work folders and opened them, hoping to find a clue.

She went through file after file on the computer and came up with nothing. She opened the drawer of his desk and shifted through the few pieces of mail from various work contacts.

Her hands drifted to a short envelope. She picked it up, turned it over and back again, studying the outside for clues. It had been mailed from Hopeton and did not have a return address.

The envelope had already been opened. She pulled out the card and opened it. A piece of paper fell out onto the desk.

Hannah frowned at the blank white card without so much as even a saying on the inside.

Confused she picked up the paper that had been inside.

The love of money is the root of all evil.

Hannah dropped the paper and pressed her fingers to her temple. Her stomach was tied in knots and she could feel a headache coming on.

James had known something was up? And he had never mentioned a thing to her? Why?

Had she been fooled by her own husband? Had she truly seen their life through rose-colored glasses?

Was she the biggest fool on the planet?

Secrets beget secrets. That's what her dad used to say. This was a big secret. A huge secret. What else had been hidden from her? Had James done what that awful text suggested? Had he taken money that wasn't his to take?

The idea curdled her insides and made her want to vomit.

Not her James. But...maybe?

If he had embezzled money, then surely she could see it on the bank accounts.

Fingers flying over the keyboard, she typed in her password.

She checked the primary bank account and then the secondary account. She went back months pouring over their statements and searching for large amounts of money that had been deposited. What she discovered was a large amount of money had been withdrawn from their savings account a few months before his passing.

Her heart lurched. It had been right around the time when their son, Gregory, had asked for help putting a down payment on his new house. But Gregory had paid the money back within a few months after getting a raise at work and the amount he'd asked for was nowhere near this amount of money. Why was this much money missing? What had James done with it? And did it have something to do with the company? It didn't make any sense.

Next Hannah pulled up the primary checking account and meticulously went through the statements.

She was about to shut the computer down when she spotted an unfamiliar account. She clicked on it, using her own password.

Access denied.

She would have to find the password. Hannah wondered if James had used a password that she would not guess. She sighed and ran her fingers through her hair and rested her elbows on the desk. Her gaze drifted over to the scrap of paper with the words.

"For the love of money is the root of all evil."

She straightened.

Hannah picked up her phone and typed the scripture in her phone.

With trembling fingers she typed in 1 Timothy 6:10 in the password.

It worked.

She pulled up the statement. There had only been one deposit made in this account for the amount of one million dollars and it had been made three months prior to James' diagnosis with cancer.

Nausea washed over her. She wanted to curl into a ball and cry.

Suddenly the doorbell rang and it jolted her out of her reality.

She didn't want visitors, not now.

Hannah quickly shut down the computer and headed to the door. She didn't bother looking to see who it was before opened the door.

Blood rushed from her face as she saw the CEO of the hospital and the other board members from the hospital standing on the other side.

None of them were smiling.

CHAPTER 11

*H*annah felt the blood drain from her face as she stared into the faces of the hospital board members. She opened her mouth but words would not come out.

Had they found out about the note? Did they know about James?

"Hannah, I can tell by the look on your face that our surprise visit has given you a giant shock." Albert clasped his hands together and looked delighted.

"You have no idea," she said quietly.

Missy, Albert's wife shoved her husband out of the way and held out her arms to Hannah. "Hannah, when Albert told me the board was coming to see you, I insisted on coming along." She gathered Hannah up in her arms and hugged her tightly. "How are you, honey?"

Hannah tried to compose herself as she hugged her back. "I'm okay, Missy." Relieved, she pulled back and forced a smile. "Thank you for making that cake. It was delicious."

Hannah shook her head and stepped out of the doorway, "Where are my manners? Please come in out of the cold."

The board members all strode in, one after another, each greeting her with a smile as they entered her home.

Hannah followed them into the living room. "Please sit," she waved her hand at the ample seating of two couches and four chairs.

"We know this is a bit of a surprise but we just wanted to drop by for a second so I could introduce the board members to you." Albert stood in front of the fireplace as if he were commanding the room.

"Yes, of course," she forced herself to relax and be cordial. "May I get anyone something to drink? A hot tea or cocoa?"

"That's very kind but no. We just came from lunch at Chastains." Albert patted his stomach.

Chastians was a high-end restaurant that usually only opened for dinner. Upon special request they could open for a group for lunch if the price was right, which it seemed it was, considering the board of twelve people had eaten there.

"Oh, yes. Chastains was always a favorite for James and myself."

Everyone nodded and murmured in agreement.

"Hannah, let me introduce you to Dr. Samuels who is our heart surgeon."

Dr. Samuels had dark hair and dark eyes, and seemed to be around fifty years old. He wore a dark tailored Armani suit. He held out his hand. "I'm so pleased to meet you Mrs. Reece."

She shook his hand and smiled. "Nice to meet you, Dr. Samuels."

"And this is our other physician on the board, Dr. Glenn. He is our oncologist," Albert smiled at the younger doctor with blonde hair and blue eyes. He looked barely old enough to vote.

"Dr. Glenn, nice to meet you," Hannah took his hand and laughed. "I do have to say, you look very young to be a doctor."

"You're not the first one to say that. In fact, I had a patient the other day who refused to be treated under me. He said he wanted to speak to the Chief of Staff. You should have seen his face when I told him he was speaking to him."

Hannah grinned.

"I keep telling Dr. Glenn he'll appreciate his youthful looks when he's fifty," Missy snickered.

"That's true. When I was twenty, James took me to an R-rated-horror movie. And they carded me to make sure I was old enough before they let me in," Hannah shook her head.

Everyone laughed.

Albert continued introducing the rest of the board. Besides the two physicians, there were two attorneys, five business owners, the mayor of Hopeton, one nurse, and a retired firefighter. There were twelve members in all.

"We can't stay but just wanted to pop over. Dr. Samuels has been wanting to meet you for a while since James generously donated so much money."

"Yes, and I can't say enough how we all feel like we made the right decision in choosing to honor James." Dr. Samuels smiled brightly.

Her expression faltered as her stomach dropped. She cleared her throat. "I'm not so sure he would want such a big fanfare."

Albert clapped his hands together. "Which is exactly why we are doing it. He was too humble when he was with us. We want the community to know how much he did," he cut his eyes at Missy and grinned, "which is why we have something special to tell you."

"You do?" she blinked.

"There will be a part of the ceremony when we will ask anyone who is willing, to share what James did for them, and how he impacted their lives," Missy grabbed her hand and squeezed. "Just imagine all the wonderful memories that will be shared that night."

Or dirty little secrets, she thought to herself.

"Oh Hannah, you don't look pleased," Missy frowned, her dark eyes searching hers.

"Oh no, it's not that. It's just. Well it's such a short notice. Will you have enough people who are willing to speak? I mean it's Christmas and some will be out of town, on vacation, or spending it with friends." She swallowed back the lump in her throat and tried to keep her expression hopeful, instead of the churning she was feeling deep inside.

"Don't you worry about a thing. We already put out the call and had so many people reply. In fact we heard back from his former business partner."

"Fred Sinclair?" her eyes widened and then she cleared her throat. "I've been trying to get in contact with him, but it seems he moved from Charleston."

"He did. He's in Charlotte and more than willing to share his memories of James at the event." Missy squealed. "Oh honey, this is going to be wonderful. You just wait and see. A real night to remember."

Hannah forced a smile. That's exactly what she was worried about.

CHAPTER 12

$\mathcal{H}$annah sipped on her morning coffee and curled up with her laptop on the couch. By the time the board members from the hospital left, her neighbor, Sarah Williams, had come over asking if she'd seen her brother Johnny. It was one distraction after another, almost as if fate were blocking her attempts at finding out the truth.

Hannah had informed Sarah she had seen Johnny on the other side of the lake riding his bike.

Since her parents had died in a plane crash, Sarah was now the legal guardian of her brother. Hannah knew there was a large age gap between the two and she had never really seen Sarah at Laurel Cove until the death of her parents. Sarah's parents, Keith and Layla Williams had been known as good neighbors on the lake and kids living around the lake could always be found at their house, hanging out and playing. It reminded Hannah of their house when Ella and Gregory were young.

Now that Sarah had come back to Hopeton, she seemed to always be chasing after her younger brother and trying to keep up with his whereabouts.

Hannah's heart tugged for the young woman who had seemed to be given such a difficult situation before she'd had time to live her life.

After Sarah left, a couple of ladies from the church dropped by asking for donations for the nursing home.

By the time she'd gotten rid of all her guests, it was after eight p.m.

Hannah decided to take a long bath and start again fresh in the morning.

She'd gotten up before her alarm went off at five thirty.

Hannah opened her laptop and typed in Fred's name. She hoped it would give her a solid tip as to whether he really still lived in North Carolina or not.

She didn't feel like driving all the way to Charlotte if it turned out to be a wild-goose chase, especially after her trip to Charleston.

Her phone buzzed. She picked it up and noticed the house cameras had captured movement on the front porch. She clicked on the camera.

Huddled on the stone steps was a small figure bundled up in a winter coat. She frowned and stood up. Her gaze flickered out to the large window. Who in the world would be outside at this hour? It was still dark outside and she certainly wasn't expecting any visitors this early.

Hannah eased to the front door and slowly opened the door.

The little head whipped around.

"Johnny. What are you doing out here? It's freezing cold." She tugged the robe tighter against her neck.

"My sister's mad at me." He said looking down. "I figured I should go somewhere while she cooled off."

Hannah bit her lip. "Well why don't you come inside? I can make you some hot chocolate."

He looked at her from under the hood of his coat. "Do you have coffee?"

She grinned. "Do you drink coffee?"

"It's usually what Sarah keeps in the house." He shrugged.

"I think you'd prefer some hot chocolate and some sugar cookies that I made yesterday."

His eyes lit up and he stood. "Okay."

Hannah grinned and held the door open wide for him to enter and then locked it once they were both inside. She walked into the living room and stood in front of the fire.

"While I make you something warm to drink, you stand in front of the fire and get warm. I don't need you getting pneumonia, especially at Christmas." She tugged off his coat and pulled the warm throw off the back of the couch and placed it around his shoulders. He sat near the blazing fire while she went into the kitchen.

She hung his coat on the back of one of the kitchen stools around the island and turned her attention to making hot chocolate.

Her heart tugged for the child who'd lost both parents at such an early age. Though she'd lost James, she still knew how blessed she was for all the time she and her children had with him. It reminded her how truly precious life was.

While the kettle heated, she pulled out her glass container of homemade sugar cookies and placed four on a Christmas plate decorated with reindeer.

"Does Sarah know you're not at home?" She looked at him staring at the fire.

He shrugged. "I don't know."

That was code for no, Sarah did not know her brother was missing.

When the kettle whistled, she poured the hot water over the mixture of hot chocolate. Normally she would make hot chocolate from scratch, but considering she needed to get something warm in Johnny fast, she went the easy route with a premade mix.

She stirred the hot chocolate thoroughly, and then placed the spoon in the sink. Picking up the mug and plate of cookies, she walked into the living room.

Hannah smiled and set them down on the coffee table. Johnny's eyes brightened when he spotted the colorful sugar cookies.

"Come sit down." She waved him over.

He sat on the edge of the couch but realized the coffee table was too far away, so he quickly settled on the floor. He took a drink of the hot chocolate and he sighed.

He looked up at her. "It's good."

"I'm glad. It should warm you back up in no time." She smiled back.

He tasted a Christmas tree sugar cookie.

"What do you think? I made those from scratch."

"I haven't had cookies this good since…" The slight smile on his lips fell away. She knew what he was going to say.

Hannah let silence drift between them for a moment while thinking how best to approach the situation.

"You know, I could give my recipe to Sarah. That way, she could make you cookies whenever you want them."

He let out an exaggerated huff as his eyes widened. "Sarah? She doesn't know how to cook. The last attempt she made, the fire alarm went off and the lasagna was burned to a crisp. It looked like something out of an alien movie."

She couldn't help but burst out laughing.

He stared at her with serious eyes.

She sobered. "You're serious."

He didn't say anything but munched on his cookies and sipped his hot chocolate.

Hannah would have to make a point of taking some meals over to Sarah, or better, invite them over for dinner.

"You know, when I first got married I didn't know

how to cook. I took some classes and now I'm pretty good at it."

"Sarah won't take classes. She would say she's too busy."

She chose her next words carefully.

"Well, I'm sure she has a lot on her plate. She has only been back in Laurel Cove for such a short time. Give her time to settle in and she'll love it as much as we do."

"I doubt it. She's either yelling at me or crying about something." He quickly finished the cookies and was taking his time on the hot chocolate, as if he had all the time in the world.

"Maybe I can help." She patted him on the shoulder. She bit back her frustration that her plans at finding Fred had been delayed once again.

"You? How can you help?" He looked up at her with a hot chocolate mustache.

Hannah couldn't help but grin. "Well, I'll bring you guys dinner twice a week. And I'll tape the recipe to the top of the container. That way if you guys like what I cook, then your sister will know how to make it."

"I don't think Sarah will do it."

"Well, encourage her. Tell her you'll help cook, too."

"Me?"

"Yes, you. You're how old now?"

"I'll be eight in the summer."

"Perfect."

"You don't think I'm too little?"

Her heart softened at his earnest expression. She wanted to put her arms around him and hug him tight.

"No. I don't think you're too little." She patted his shoulder. "Now drink up and I'll drive you back home. But I do need to text Sarah so she won't worry."

"Do you have to? She's going to be mad." He frowned.

"I do. And I promise she won't be mad."

He nodded while she sent a quick text to her neighbor, promising her that Johnny was okay and she would bring him home.

CHAPTER 13

*A*fter she'd taken Johnny back home, Hannah showered and dressed for the day. She'd found an address for Fred in Charlotte and she intended to drive over there to confront him about the letters. Even if he wasn't the one sending the letters, he might be able to shed some light on whether the accusations were true or not.

If anyone knew James it would be his best friend, Fred.

Hannah glanced at her reflection in the mirror. Her white cashmere sweater complimented her black skinny jeans and tall black boots. She pulled her red wool coat out of the closet and slipped it on.

It would take about two and a half hours to get to Charlotte from Hopeton. She needed to get on the road.

Hannah hooked her purse on her shoulder and opened the door.

She froze.

Carolina stood there without a coat, shaking and crying. "Hannah, you have to help me."

"Oh my gosh. Where's your coat? Carolina, are you hurt?" Hannah grabbed her friend by the shoulders.

Carolina shook her head. "It's not me. It's…", she choked back a sob, "it's Phoenix."

Hannah's heart nearly stopped. "Did he get hit?" While the majority of the neighbors on Laurel Cove drove slowly, there were a few that had teenage drivers that were known to have a heavy foot. She'd almost had to take a ditch when one teenage girl had crossed into her lane while she was texting.

Carolina shook her head. "No. We were walking down the road and he suddenly fell over at the end of your driveway. I tried to get him to walk but it's like his back legs won't work. He's breathing heavy and his eyes are weird, going side to side really fast. I think he's dying. I couldn't carry him because he's too heavy. Oh, Hannah. I've got to get back to him. He's probably scared."

"Okay, calm down." Hannah glanced at the time on her watch before she put her arms around Carolina's shoulder. "Let's get him in my car and we'll take him to the vet. Okay?"

Carolina was still shaking but managed to give Hannah a nod.

Hannah led her friend to her car and helped her in the passenger's seat before getting into the driver's seat.

Hannah drove slowly down her driveway. She

spotted Phoenix by her mailbox. Sweet Carolina had taken off her coat and put it over the dog to keep him warm.

Carolina was out of the car first. She was on her knees hovering over the dog who looked like he was either having a seizure or a stroke.

Hannah popped her trunk and pulled out a blanket she kept for emergencies. James had told her once to keep some granola bars, water, and a blanket in her trunk in case she ever got caught on the interstate and a winter storm rolled in.

She smiled, grateful she had the blanket for Phoenix.

"Take your coat off and let's put the blanket around him before we pick him up."

Carolina nodded and put her coat on.

Hannah knelt beside her friend. Then they both picked up the dog. They carried him carefully to the car where Carolina sat and Hannah helped get the dog situated in her lap.

"Oh Hannah, he's shaking so hard," Carolina said tearfully.

"Let's get him to the vet." Hannah put the car in gear and looked over at her. "What vet do you use?"

"I've not had time to take him. The farm supply had a weekend where they were giving vaccines to dogs so I just had them do his shots." Carolina's lip quivered.

"Not a problem." She stopped at a stop sign and sent a quick text to Elena, asking her which vet she used for Lawrence.

"Dr. Barnaby." Hannah looked at the text. She looked at Carolina. "Ever heard of him? He's off Vine Street."

"I think Getty mentioned Dr. Barnaby when I was asking about vets in Hopeton."

"Well, if Elena takes Lawrence to him, then he has to be the best." Hannah gave her a reassuring smile.

Within minutes, they were at Dr. Barnaby's office. Seeing the serious situation, they rushed them into the room where they took blood samples. Dr. Barnaby came in and examined Phoenix.

"Let's see what's going on, buddy." Dr. Barnaby smiled and gently examined the dog.

"We're going to give Phoenix some medicine to calm him down. From his symptoms, I think he's had either a stroke or a seizure. We need to keep him here overnight for observation."

"Will he be by himself?" Carolina asked.

"No, we have a tech that stays overnight and if the situation looks serious then I'll stay here as well." Barnaby assured her. "Don't worry, Mrs. Johnson. Phoenix is in good hands."

A tech came in with a syringe and a small bottle. He handed it to Dr. Barnaby.

Hannah squeezed Carolina's hand when the doctor gave Phoenix the shot. The dog didn't even whimper.

Carolina walked over and cradled the dog's face in her hands. She kissed the top of his head. "I love you, Phoenix."

The dog's breathing had slowed some and he seemed calmer.

"Mrs. Johnson, we will call you if there is any change in Phoenix's condition." Dr. Barnaby gave her a reassuring smile.

"Thank you." Carolina nodded and collected her coat and stuffed her hands in her pockets. She frowned. "I forgot my cell phone. What if his condition worsens on our way back?" She looked at Hannah.

Hannah looked at Dr. Barnaby. "Can you add my number to his file?"

"Of course." He pulled out a pen from his white-lab-jacket pocket and wrote down Hannah's number as she spoke.

"Again, thank you." Carolina gave the vet one last teary-eyed look before hugging Phoenix tight before they left the room.

CHAPTER 14

*H*annah held Carolina's elbow as they walked down the hallway to the exit. "I have a good feeling that he will be okay," she gave her arm a reassuring squeeze.

Carolina swiped at the tears from her eyes and gave Hannah a sad smile. "I hope you're right. And thanks for bringing us here. I guess we spoiled any plans you had this morning."

Hannah glanced at the time on her watch. "I was just going to make a trip over to Charlotte." She glanced over at Carolina. Her heart tugged for her friend. "Why don't you go with me?"

Carolina glanced down at her yoga pants, sweat-shirt, and Ugg boots. "In this?"

Hannah shrugged. "Sure, why not?"

"Because I look like I'm headed to the gym, while you look like you're headed off to 'lunch with the ladies.'"

Hannah let out a laugh. "I'm not headed off to 'lunch with the ladies', as you put it." Her smile faltered.

"Are you going to do some Christmas shopping?" Carolina snuggled down into her coat.

"Not exactly."

Carolina's eyes grew wide as she stared at Hannah. "Are you meeting a date?"

Hannah jerked her head over at Carolina and gaped. "What?! No. Why would you think that?"

Carolina sighed. "I don't know. Just hoping to have someone to double date with me and Thomas, I suppose."

Hannah tightened her grip on the steering wheel. "If I tell you something, will you promise not to say a word to anyone?"

"Of course."

"I mean it. Not even to Bernice." She leveled a glare at her.

"Bernice is the last person I would confide in, not that I would tell her anything we talk about. I hope you know that." Carolina looked at her earnestly.

" I do. It's just … well, this is a serious situation." Hannah turned onto the highway heading to Charlotte.

"I can tell by the way you're being so… secretive." Carolina reached over and touched her shoulder. "Is everything okay?"

"I don't know. That's what I'm trying to find out." Hannah kept her eyes on the road as she dug around in her purse for the first letter she'd received. She pulled it out, glanced at it and then handed it to Carolina. "Here, read this."

Carolina took the paper and opened it up to read it. "Hannah! Who sent this thing?"

"I don't know. That's what I've been trying to find out. And that's why we are going to Charlotte."

"This is blackmail. And I'm sure it's not true. How awful for someone to try to take advantage of a widow." Carolina shook her head.

"Is it?" Hannah asked softly. "How do I know it's not true? How do I know that my marriage to James was not built on a lie?" She glanced over at her friend and then back at the road.

"Oh. Now I understand." Carolina nodded. "That's why you were asking me all those questions about red flags and Chris."

Hannah could do nothing but nod.

"Hannah, I just don't think James could do something like this," she sighed, "but then again, I didn't know the man nor am I a good judge of character." She looked over at her. "Did you take the letter to the police?"

"No!" Hannah said a little too quickly. She shook her head and took a deep breath before blowing it out. "I don't want to go to them until I have more information. If it's false, then someone is trying to ruin James' reputation and hurt me and the kids. If it's true, then there will be legal ramifications and it will hurt the kids."

"That's a hard situation to be in." Carolina frowned. "I'll do anything I can to help."

Hannah cut her eyes at her. "Really?"

"Of course. You're my friend and I'm here to help." Carolina brightened for the first time since leaving Phoenix at the vet.

"I'll take you up on that. Right now, we are headed to Charlotte to see if I can find Fred Sinclair, James' partner before leaving Stars Global and his best friend. If anyone knew that James was doing something illegal then it would have been Fred."

"If they were best friends, then why did he leave the company? Did they have a falling out?" Carolina frowned.

"That's the thing. When James told me Fred was leaving Stars Global, I was stunned. I asked if they had a disagreement and he insisted that they had not. James said Fred was leaving to venture out to other business opportunities."

Carolina stared at her. "You think he was lying?"

"Looking back now, I wonder if maybe Fred had found out something that had upset him and decided to leave."

"That's one explanation." Carolina cringed.

"Right now, I'm afraid it's the most likely scenario that fits." Hannah tightened her fingers on the steering wheel as her stomach did a free fall. Who knew what they were going to discover that day?

CHAPTER 15

*A*fter a quick stop at a drive-through to pick up some lunch, Hannah and Carolina pulled into the small suburb of Charlotte. The neighborhood was older with unassuming homes dating in the eighties.

"I didn't think this is where Fred would be living. When he was living in Hopeton, he had a nice house in Garden Gate."

Garden Gate was a gated neighborhood that had a stunning golf course. Fred's three-story home was one of the finest in the area.

"You didn't mention a wife. Did Fred never marry?"

Hannah turned and glanced over at Carolina. "He was married to Lydia, but they divorced soon after James and Fred started Stars Global. They never really seemed to be a good fit as a couple."

"What do you mean?" Carolina asked.

"Every time we went out to dinner, Lydia never went. Fred was always making an excuse for her. She would have a headache, or she was out of town with her mom, or she had another engagement." Hannah frowned. "Fred had us over for dinner at his house and even then, Lydia wouldn't be there. It was like they were more or less roommates."

"How odd."

"I certainly thought so. When I asked James about the situation, he said that some couples weren't as fortunate as us," Hannah sighed.

"Look, someone is having a yard sale." Carolina pointed to the house on the left with a driveway full of items for sale. "I might have to take a peek before we leave."

Hannah chuckled and shook her head. When the navigation system informed said they had reached their destination, her stomach tightened with dread.

She stopped in front of a white house with a tiny porch and a carport.

Hannah shook her head. "This can't be right. This house is too…"

"Modest?" Carolina offered.

Hannah nodded. "Yes. And Fred was anything but modest."

"Well, we might as well go see if he's home." Carolina reached for the door handle.

Hannah suddenly grabbed her arm, stopping her. "Carolina, I'm afraid of what I'm about to find out," she admitted, her voice trembling ever so slightly.

Carolina patted Hannah's hand and smiled. "Whatever it is, I'll face it with you, and you will get through this, okay?"

Hannah quietly nodded, took a deep breath and got out of the car. She walked around and met Carolina on the dingy sidewalk.

"I'll go up and knock. You wait here." Hannah stared at the house.

"You've got this, Hannah," Carolina reassured.

On shaky legs, Hannah made her way up the walkway to the door. For some reason her footsteps seemed to echo loudly and she wondered if Carolina could hear her heart pounding in her chest like a jackhammer.

Reaching the door, she steadied herself and then knocked.

Seconds seemed to stretch to eternity as she waited.

When no one answered, she knocked again, this time louder and longer.

"I don't think he's home." Carolina appeared at her elbow.

Hannah nearly jumped out of her skin. She'd been so concentrated on the door opening that she hadn't heard Carolina approach.

Hannah turned to the empty carport. "You're probably right. There's no car. He's probably at work. It is in the middle of the day."

"Can I help you two ladies?" An elderly woman called out from the sidewalk behind them. They both turned. She still had her hair in pink curlers and had a brightly colored quilt thrown across her shoulders.

Hannah froze. She took a step toward the woman and opened her mouth.

"Are you two here from the church to pick up the table for bingo?" the old woman asked.

"Yes, yes we are." Carolina spoke without missing a beat.

"What are you doing?" Hannah muttered under her breath.

"We are going to get inside and have a look around. Just follow my lead," Carolina said under her breath.

"Hi, I'm Bernice and this is Patty," Carolina walked up to the old woman and smiled.

The old lady narrowed her eyes at the pair. "I'm Elizabeth Holstein. I'm Fred's neighbor. I look after his house when he's not here."

"Do you expect him back soon?" Hannah asked.

"No." Elizabeth looked Hannah up and down. "Say, you don't look much like a Patty. You're too fancy for a name like that."

"Oh really?" Hannah chuckled in spite of her nerves. "What do I look like?"

"You look like a Morgan. Maybe a Lisa." Elizabeth nodded.

"What about me?" Carolina asked brightly. "Do I look like a Bernice?"

"Yes," the woman deadpanned.

Carolina scowled.

"We were really hoping Fred would be home. You know, so we could get the table," Hannah swallowed down the lie.

"Not a problem. Just use the key under the mat and let yourselves in. Fred said someone from the church would drop by. Replace the key and lock up when you leave."

"That's not very safe, you know. Keeping a key under the mat." Carolina frowned.

Elizabeth barked out a laugh. "Honey, you can't steal from the poor." She tightened the quilt around her shoulders and toddled back down the sidewalk.

They waited until she disappeared into her house before walking back up to the door.

Can't steal from the poor?

Perhaps, but someone is stealing from the corporation's bank account.

CHAPTER 16

*H*annah knelt and quickly found the key under the mat. With nerves on high alert, she glanced over her shoulder before sticking the key in the lock.

She turned the knob and they both stepped inside.

"Hannah, be honest," Carolina grabbed her by the shoulders, "Do I look like a Bernice?"

Hannah chortled. "No. You don't look like a Bernice."

"What do I look like?"

"You look like a Carolina." Hannah walked further into the sparsely decorated house. The walls were white, and the floors were hardwood and had to be over forty years old.

There were no pictures on the wall, only a couch and recliner in the living room along with a TV mounted on the wall.

"Fred certainly isn't into decorating."

"Which is weird. In Hopeton, he paid an expensive interior designer to decorate his house. And he had a lot of expensive art work he displayed. This," she waved her hand around the room, "isn't normal for him."

"Something really bad must have happened if he doesn't have any money." Carolina said as they entered the kitchen.

"I just hope that whatever it was doesn't involve James." Hannah muttered as she opened the refrigerator. "There's sandwich meat and some leftover Chinese food. Not exactly caviar and champagne." She looked at Carolina.

"That's what a single man normally exists on. I wouldn't worry too much." Carolina shrugged and walked down the hallway to the bedroom. Hannah followed.

"Check out the bedroom," Carolina moved to the side so Hannah could walk in first.

There was only a mattress on the floor and a small bedside table with a Bible and a lamp. A chest of drawers sat beside a closet door. The walls, like the rest of the house, were void of pictures or anything personal.

Hannah left the bedroom and opened the door to another room in the hallway.

It was a second bedroom which was being used as an office. There was a desk, printer, and filing cabinet.

Hannah looked over her shoulder at Carolina. "Bingo."

Hannah stepped inside and looked at the small desk. "There's no computer. Bet he has a laptop and he's taken it with him."

"Maybe we can find some papers, maybe a bank statement. You don't think there are any hidden cameras anywhere do you?" Carolina clasped her hands together.

"There's no place to hide a camera. This place is as bare as they come. I think we're pretty safe. Look in the filing cabinet and I'll check the closet."

Carolina knelt beside the filing cabinet and began looking through the papers.

Hannah went over to a closet and opened it. There were boxes upon boxes which were dated with the month and the year.

She pulled one down that had the month when Fred still worked at Stars Global.

She sat on the hardwood floor and crossed her legs before pulling the lid off the box.

Inside were copies of invoices and receipts from clients of Stars Global. She frowned. "Why did he keep copies of invoices and receipts?"

Carolina looked over her shoulder and shrugged. "I don't know. I'm not a business woman. I just like gardening."

"Ah, but you are a business woman, Carolina. You just don't know it." Hannah smiled.

"What do you mean?" Carolina stopped going through the papers and turned to look at her.

"I mean, you are the reason Bernice's nursery is

doing so well. Before you came along, I thought she was going to sell. But with your ideas and your hard work, the nursery is booming. Ideas, and implementing them are what business men and women do best."

Carolina smiled and thrust her shoulders back. "Yeah. Maybe I am a business woman." With renewed vigor she went back to investigating the files.

Hannah pulled out a large envelope and pulled out the contents. "This is paperwork regarding Fred leaving the company."

Carolina stopped what she was doing and went to sit next to Hannah. "What does it say?"

Hannah scanned the documents. "It's a legal agreement that states Fred voluntarily leaves Stars Global and sells his shares to James. It also states that he received a very nice severance package."

"Then why is he living here?" Carolina frowned.

"Good question." Hannah flipped through the paperwork and then froze when she came to a handwritten note to James from Fred.

"He wrote James a note." Hannah blinked.

"What does it say?"

Hannah blinked back the tears. *"James, we've been friends for too long for this to pull us apart. Think of the company. Please I beg you to reconsider and do the right thing." ~Fred*

Silence stretched between them.

Carolina cleared her throat. "Did James ever give a reason why Fred left the company? I mean they were making good money. Why would anyone want to leave a job like that and end up," Carolina looked around, "here."

Hannah blinked back tears. "Maybe he didn't want to leave. Maybe he found out about the money and James forced him out before he could tell anyone."

"It's still not definite proof. What you need to do is talk to Fred face-to-face. Until you do, let's make a copy of that paper." Carolina took all the contents of the envelope and began making copies on the printer.

Hannah felt the room begin to shrink and she stood. She had to get some fresh air before she passed out.

She headed into the kitchen and out the back door. There was no deck just steps leading out into the fenced-in yard. She walked out into the middle of the yard and lifted her face to the sun and closed her eyes.

"What am I going to do?" She said to herself. "How do I tell my children?"

"Just tell them." A male voice on the other side of the fence called out.

Hannah jumped and looked around and froze. A man in his late sixties on the other side was repairing a broken board. He wore a flannel jacket and blue jeans with a tool belt strapped around his waist. In his gloved hand was a hammer.

"Excuse me?" Hannah narrowed her eyes.

"Oh, I thought you were talking to me. Asking me for advice." The man put a nail in his mouth and held up a board. "You'd be surprised how many strangers ask their handyman for advice."

"I suppose I would." She glanced around. "You haven't seen Fred have you?"

"Is that the gentleman that lives there?" The man shook his head. "No. I haven't seen anyone in that backyard except for you. It's too bad, too. It could be a really nice outdoor space if someone built a deck, put some lawn furniture out, maybe set up a firepit." He pointed with his hammer. "He's the only one on this street with such a large oak tree. I can imagine some nice backyard BBQs in the summer under it."

She turned and stared at the tree. "Yes, you're right. I guess Fred has other things on his mind."

She looked back at him. "I'm H…..Patty." She almost forgot and used her real name.

"Nice to meet you Patty. I'm Nelson. I live a few houses down. Just fixing this area of the fence for Mrs. Wimble. Her sons live out of state and I help look after her."

"That's very kind of you." Hannah walked closer to the fence. "I don't suppose you know Fred."

"Oh a little. We have a street party in the spring and in the fall. Everyone sets up a table and brings a potluck. I usually make my chili for chili dogs. I think he came to that one."

She frowned. "Was he by himself?"

The man studied her, as if trying to figure her out.

"I'm sorry for so many questions. Fred used to work with my husband. They owned a business together."

"You don't say." Nelson cocked his head. "I wouldn't have figured him for a businessman. He's so …humble."

She blinked. Humble? That was the last word she would use to describe Fred Sinclair.

"Really? So Nelson, do you know what kind of work he does now?"

"He's at the church most days, volunteering I think. But he's not there now. He told Elizabeth he was going out of town. Should be back in a few weeks, I think."

"Hannah!" Carolina stepped out the back door and then froze when she spotted Nelson. "I mean Patty. It's time to go."

"Hannah?" Nelson arched a brow.

"That's my friend, Bernice. She has ten kids and one is named Hannah. She sometimes calls me all their names before she gets to mine." Hannah gave a shaky laugh.

"I can understand that. I only have six kids. Twelve grandkids. I sometimes call the roll, too."

"Nice meeting you, Nelson." Hannah waved and hurried back to the house. Once inside she locked the door.

"Did you get everything copied?" Hannah took the papers that Carolina held out.

"Yes. And everything is back in its place. If we leave now, then we can make it back to Hopeton before the snow starts. I've been looking at the weather app and there's another winter storm headed for us."

Hannah nodded and followed Carolina to the front door. "Wait. I forgot one more thing." She left Carolina at the front door and headed back into the office. She found a blank piece of paper and a pen.

She quickly scribbled a message and on her way out she stuck it on his front door with some tape she'd found in a drawer.

Fred, I need to talk to you, face-to-face. This is important. ~Hannah

She didn't write her last name, she didn't need to. Fred had once told her that she was the only Hannah that he'd ever met.

He'd know who it was from. And knowing him, he'd come find her.

CHAPTER 17

*H*annah and Carolina drove back to Hopeton in silence. The vet had called with an update on Phoenix, advising the dog was going to make a full recovery and could be picked up in the morning.

By the time Hannah pulled into Carolina's driveway, the winter storm was in full force.

Snow was coming down hard and fast, making visibility difficult. In the morning, a fresh blanket of snow would be covering all the front lawns of the homes on the lake.

Hannah thanked Carolina for everything and drove back to her own home.

Relief settled over her as she drove up the snow-covered driveway. The outdoor lighting on the house gave the place a cozy feel and she couldn't wait to get inside out of the snowstorm.

Inside she went to her bedroom and changed into

some black yoga pants with a pink sweater. Slipping on her fuzzy boots, she headed into the kitchen and opened the refrigerator.

Today was a lot of firsts for her, and not in a good way. Breaking and entering, lying to gain access to someone's house, and even using a different name.

Hannah shook her head. The whole thing made her sick.

Her stomach rumbled, reminding her it was dinnertime.

She pulled out some salmon and quickly heated up the oven. She preferred to cook in the outdoor kitchen but with the winter storm upon her she decided to stay inside and use her oven.

She added some melted butter, salt and pepper, and lemon to the salmon before popping it in the oven. She made a fresh salad out of spinach, tomatoes, cucumbers, and onions tossed in a homemade balsamic dressing. She placed the salad inside the refrigerator while the fish cooked.

While she waited, she went into the wine cellar and chose a chilled chardonnay. She rarely drank, but tonight she needed something to calm her nerves.

Maybe she should call the police and tell them about the letters. If she did, and it turned out to be true, what kind of fate would she or her kids be facing? What kind of repercussions could this mean for Gregory and Ella? Could they lose their part in the business? Would they have to repay the money taken? She just didn't know.

She found the electric wine opener and opened the wine.

She poured some of the chardonnay into the crystal wine glass and headed to the living room.

Hannah held up the remote control and pushed the button to start the fire.

She curled up on the couch watching the flames while sipping on her wine.

When the oven buzzed, letting her know the salmon was done, she got up and headed back to the kitchen.

She fixed her plate and headed into the dining room. She pulled out the large chair to the side and stopped.

James always sat at the head of the table.

Hannah shoved the chair back in place and pulled out the chair at the head of the table.

Sitting down, she face the large window over the lake.

In silent contemplation she ate her dinner.

How could James have done this to her? To the children? To the business he claimed to love? What about the employees?

As she was cleaning up the kitchen, her phone rang.

Hannah dried her hands on the dish towel and picked up her phone. She smiled when she saw it was Gregory calling.

"Hello, Babe. Merry Christmas."

"Merry Christmas, Mom." He chuckled. "Sorry, I haven't called before now. It's been crazy at work. My new client is keeping me busy and he's already recommended me to two other friends of his who are moving to the city."

"That's wonderful, Son." She smiled. "You are certainly climbing the ladder of success. I'm so proud," she pressed her lips together and added, "your father would be proud, too."

"Thanks, Mom. That means a lot." He said softly.

"How's Shelia?"

"She's great. She loves being off during the Christmas holidays. Maybe I should have been a teacher instead of an architect."

Hannah laughed. "I think you are both doing what you were meant to do."

"I guess you're right," he agreed "I got my tux cleaned for Dad's dedication ceremony. Shelia wants to know what color dress you are wearing. She said she wasn't sure if the girls were supposed to coordinate or not."

"I've not thought of that, but it would be nice. I bought a red dress. I'll text her the pictures and call her to see if she and Ella would like to all wear red."

"Yeah, do that. The last time I told her the dress code for a client's cocktail party was white, she ended up being the only woman wearing white. The rest of the women were wearing off-white, or so she informed me in no uncertain terms." He chuckled. "I thought white was white."

"You have a lot to learn about cocktail parties." She laughed.

"And women" he added. "How's everything else going?"

How much should she tell him? She didn't doubt her husband's love for his children. And she wasn't one-hundred-percent sure James had taken the money. She just didn't know how much she should divulge to her son.

"Fine," she finally said.

"Doesn't sound like everything is fine." He lowered his voice. "Ella called and said she spoke to you a few days ago. She said you sounded off and told her you couldn't talk long."

She bit her lip. The pressure was on to come clean. "Sorry, honey. I was driving. I'll call her back tonight so she doesn't worry."

"Mom?"

"Yes?"

"I know you. I know when something is wrong. You don't sound like yourself. Spill it."

She took a deep breath and then released. Okay, the gig was up. She could no longer hide from her son. Like he said, he knew her entirely too well.

"I was going to talk to you about it when you came for Christmas. Perhaps I should tell you now."

"What?" His voice was tense, on edge.

"I've been getting some letters."

"Letters? What kind of letters? And from who?"

"I don't know who they are from. There's no return address and there's no name."

"Again, what kind of letters?"

"The first one said some very disparaging things about your father."

"Like what?" His voice grew louder.

"It said that I didn't know James like I thought I did and that they were going to tell the whole world unless I paid them money."

"Mom! You should have told me. Did you go to the police?"

"No! And I'm not going to until I have more to go on. I'm only telling you because…"

"You don't believe what they are claiming about Dad, do you?"

"No, of course not. It's just…"

"Then what is it?"

"I want to talk to Fred first."

"Fred Sinclair? I thought he moved away, to Charleston, I think."

"How'd you know that? I had to track his address down from Terri."

"He sent me a sympathy card. Right after Dad died."

"Really?" She frowned.

"Yeah, didn't you get one?"

"Not that I recall. But to be honest, I wasn't very attentive to who sent what at that particular time. I was still trying to grapple with the fact your dad was gone."

"He loved you a lot, you know."

"I know." Her voice was tiny and small and she felt awful that she had even brought this whole thing up to Gregory.

"Look, if you get any more letters, call me immediately. We'll take them to the police. I don't know who's trying to intimidate you, but it's not legal. Extortion is a crime. And preying on a widow is a sin. Just remember that."

"I will." She nodded her head. "I'll let you go. I know you're busy. Can't wait to see you both."

"Love you, too, Mom."

"I love you, too, Son."

CHAPTER 18

The next morning, Hannah woke up but didn't get out of bed immediately. She stared up at the ceiling, wondering if Gregory was right. Should she go to the police?

She hadn't told her daughter, Ella, about the letters and as far as she was concerned she wasn't going to. Not until she arrived home. She didn't want her to worry needlessly about something that may, or may not, be true.

Hannah thought she'd become pretty good at protecting her kids, but after her conversation with Gregory, she realized he'd gotten the truth out of her more easily than she liked to admit.

Her strong façade was starting to crack.

She threw back the covers and headed straight for the bathroom. What she needed was a long hot shower to clear her head.

By the time she got out and threw on her robe, she

was dying for a cup of coffee.

Her hair hung in wet tendrils around her shoulder as she padded into the kitchen.

She pulled her favorite coffee mug out of the cabinet and set it under the gourmet coffee machine. She pressed a few buttons and within seconds the scent of freshly-ground coffee wafted up to her nose.

The sun was just starting to come up over the lake as she sat down on the couch with her mug.

She lifted the mug to her lips and froze.

The creak of a door had her heart pounding in her chest.

Now she was imagining things. She shook her head.

Until she heard soft footsteps in the foyer.

She set the coffee cup down on the coffee table and glanced around frantically for some kind of weapon.

When she didn't find anything to use, she dropped to the floor and began crawling to the kitchen for a knife.

"Mom, what are you doing crawling on the floor?" Ella dropped her suitcase on the floor and eyed her mother as if she had lost her marbles. "Are you okay?"

"Ella." Hannah sat back on her heels and looked up at the ceiling, trying to calm her breath. "You scared the crap out of me. I thought you were a burglar."

"A burglar that has a key?" Ella arched her perfect eyebrow. She grimaced. "Sorry, Mom. I didn't mean to scare you. I got up early so I could have the first cup of coffee with you." She held out her hands and helped Hannah up. "I didn't mean to give you a heart attack."

Hannah laughed and pulled her daughter into a tight hug. "I'm so glad you're here." When she let her go, she patted her hand. "Come on, let's get you that coffee."

After they settled onto the couch with their coffee, Ella began giving Hannah the update on her life.

The job was going well, the love life sucked.

Ella sighed. "It's just as well, that me and Ethan broke up. We just wanted different things." She shrugged. "Besides, I want to focus on my work."

"There's no rush to settle down honey. You're still young."

"I'm only a year younger than Gregory and he's already married with the big house. Next will be babies." Ella rolled her eyes.

Hannah grinned. "I can't wait."

"I know you can't." Ella laughed at her mother. "You'll have those kids so spoiled they'll never want to go back to Shelia and Gregory's house."

They both laughed in agreement.

"How are things here?" Ella looked from the large fireplace out the window overlooking the lake. "It feels like I've been gone too long. It seems like I can still feel Dad in this place. Like he's just sleeping in and he'll be out any minute wanting to make pancakes and go build a snowman." A sad look crossed her face.

Hannah reached over and squeezed her hand. "I know, honey." She looked around the room built on memories and love to last a lifetime. "I miss him so much."

Ella blinked back tears and nodded. "Let's change the subject. It's too early for tears."

"Fine. What do you want to talk about?" Hannah lifted the cup to her lips and took a sip.

"Tell me about the letters."

Hannah choked on her coffee.

Ella patted her on the back. "Sorry. I thought Gregory told you he was going to call me."

Hannah wiped her lips and narrowed her eyes. "Well, he didn't. What all did Gregory say?"

"Not much, you know how he is. He just said some creep has been sending you disturbing letters."

"Disturbing?"

"Yeah, he didn't go into detail. But if someone is sending you…perverted letters, you should go to the police. I think it could be a stalker."

"A stalker?" Hannah blinked. She was grateful that Gregory hadn't told Ella the letters were regarding her father. But she certainly didn't want Ella to start worrying over her having an imaginary stalker.

"Stalking is a crime, you know." She crossed her arms. "Now everything makes sense. That's why you were so jumpy when I came in. You thought the stalker had found his way inside your house."

Hannah gave her daughter a reassuring smile. "Honey, I don't want you to worry about me or anything else."

"I won't. You know why? Because we are going to the pawn shop and you are buying a gun."

CHAPTER 19

"*A* gun? I've never shot a gun in my life." Hannah stood up and headed into the kitchen. Ella was clearly taking this too far.

"I have a gun. Every woman should be able to protect herself, especially single women." Ella trailed behind her, knotting her long blonde hair into a messy bun at the back of her neck. She slid onto a barstool at the kitchen island while Hannah fixed herself another cup of coffee.

"You are different. You are a single woman living away from home. You need protection."

"And so do you." Ella countered. "That's why we are going to cancel any plans you have today. After you get ready, we are headed to the pawn shop. She stood and headed to her old room.

Hannah buried her face in her hands. She needed an out.

She headed into her room and found her cell phone.

She quickly phoned Carolina and explained the situation.

"I'll be there in thirty minutes," Carolina said before she hung up.

Hannah took her time drying her hair and putting on makeup. By the time that was done, she didn't hurry when she went to her closet to select an outfit.

What did one wear to purchase a weapon, she thought dryly.

Just as she was slipping on some ballet flats, the doorbell rang.

Hannah hurried to the door but Ella beat her to it.

Her daughter peeked through the glass and then opened the door.

"Can I help you?" Ella cocked her head.

"Carolina, come in," Hannah opened the door wide. "Ella, this is my neighbor Carolina Johnson. She just moved into the pretty lake house that has the great oak tree in the back."

"Oh, yes. I loved that backyard as a child." Ella smiled and held out her hand. "I'm Ella Reece. It's a pleasure to meet you."

Carolina smiled brightly. "Oh Ella, it's wonderful to finally meet you. Your mother talks about you and Gregory all the time. And you are just as stunning as your mother."

"You're very sweet. Thank you." Ella blushed.

"I'm so sorry to barge in like this, but you are my only hope, Hannah."

Hannah's spirits lifted. "Of course. What do you need? I'm here to help."

"Well, it's Phoenix."

"Is he okay? I thought he came home from the vet."

"Yes, he's home and doing better." Carolina slid her gaze over to Ella. "My dog, Phoenix had a stroke and Hannah was kind enough to drive us to the vet to get him checked out."

"I'm so sorry to hear that." Ella gave her a sympathetic look.

"Yes, well. Bernice insists that I come in to work today, and I am still afraid to leave Phoenix alone." Carolina slid her gaze to Hannah.

"Bernice? The woman that owns the nursery in town?" Ella frowned.

"Yes, that's the one. Anyway, I was wondering if you could watch him while I'm at work." Carolina looked uneasy as she looked between the two women, like she hated to impose.

"Of course. I've got nothing planned today." Hannah smiled brightly. Thank God for Carolina.

"Well actually..." Ella started to speak but Hannah cut her off.

"Do you want me to come get him?" Hannah asked quickly.

"No need. He's in the car. Just in case you said yes."

"Perfect." Hannah clasped her hands together. "Do you need help getting him out of the car?"

"No, he's walking now. But he does stumble. The vet seems to think he'll get better and then plateau off to a degree. He's not really a bother. Just sleeps a lot. He'll need to be walked around ten. His medicine makes him go to the bathroom more frequently."

Hannah nodded. "Just bring him in. I'll put him by the fireplace so he can look out the window."

"You're a lifesaver, Hannah," Carolina gave a strained smile to Ella.

Hannah left the door open and opened the foyer closet. She found a couple of soft blankets and headed into the living room.

"Mom, are you sure this is a good idea?" Ella followed her. "What if he gets sick or has another stroke?"

"Then I'll take him to the vet, Ella." She shook her head. "You act like I don't know how to take care of an animal."

"We never had a dog when we were little. It just seems out of character for you to be taking care of a dog now." Ella eyed her mother.

"Here we go," Carolina urged Phoenix into the living room.

He was walking on his own but staggered every three steps he took.

"Oh Phoenix." Hannah knelt down. The dog looked at her with his head in a slight tilt.

"He tends to veer to the left when he walks sometimes. So when you walk him, make sure he doesn't get too close to the lake." Carolina bit her lip.

Phoenix finally made it to the bed of blankets and curled up in a ball.

Hannah petted the dog. "You poor thing. You just need some rest and you'll be back to chasing squirrels and deer."

"He's already eaten so you don't have to worry about feeding him." Carolina bent, cupped Phoenix's face between her hands and kissed the dog. "You be good for Hannah."

"Can I give him a snack?" Hannah stood.

"Sure," Carolina snapped her fingers and cringed, "I knew I was forgetting something. His water bowl."

"No worries, I have a bowl that will work," Hannah reassured her friend. She put her arm across Carolina's shoulders and walked her to the front door. "I'll take good care of your baby."

Carolina looked over Hannah's shoulder and lowered her voice. "I don't think Ella is very happy about all this."

"She'll get over it," Hannah muttered. "The last thing I want to do is go gun shopping."

Carolina's eyes widened. "A gun? What prompted that?"

"She thinks the letters I've been getting are from a stalker." Hannah shook her head.

"You should tell her the whole story, Hannah."

"I'm too far in right now. Once I have all the puzzle pieces I'll tell her. No need for her to worry as well."

Carolina gave her a doubtful look. "Call me if you have any questions. I'll have my phone on me."

"I will, and believe me, you're actually doing me a favor." Hannah gave her friend a grateful smile.

CHAPTER 20

"*How* about some breakfast?" Hannah said, trying to act cheerfully. She pulled the glass container of pancake mix out of the pantry. She found her large bowl and measured out enough for the both of them.

Ella sighed. "I was really hoping to get you to the pawn shop this morning. They'll probably be closed before Carolina gets home to pick up Phoenix. And they are closed tomorrow."

"Good," Hannah muttered and cracked a couple of eggs into the mixture.

"What was that?" Ella cocked her head.

"Oh nothing. Just trying to make a mental list of what we need to do before your father's dedication ceremony." She poured some fresh milk into the mix and stirred slowly.

"About that. It's only a few days away. I'm surprised they are able to pull something together so quickly." Ella settled on the couch and pulled out her phone.

Hannah nodded. "I was assured everything is being handled. Knowing Missy, she will light a fire under Albert and the others to make sure it turns out perfectly. All we need to do is show up in our cocktail attire."

"Yes, I almost forgot to tell you," Ella stopped checking her email long enough to make eye contact with her mother, "I found a dress. But they didn't have it in my size. So they are having it ordered from another store and having it shipped here."

"Perfect. I can't wait to see it. Do you have a picture?" Hannah stopped what she was doing and went to sit beside Ella.

"I do." Ella swiped her finger across her phone and pulled up her photos. She kept scrolling until she found what she was looking for. "It's red." She smiled and held out the phone to her mother.

Hannah took the phone and smiled. "Ella, it's beautiful. That V-neck will look great on you."

"Before you say how cold I'll get because it has spaghetti straps, I plan to wear the fur cape I picked up in New York last year. It's perfect."

"That will look great." Hannah smiled. "I hope Shelia finds a dress in time."

Ella laughed. "I wouldn't worry about that. Gregory's new client has been hooking him up with all his rich friends. One of them is a fashion designer, by the name of Delphine. Gregory let it slip that our father is being honored at a dedication ceremony and his client insisted that Shelia let Delphine dress her."

"That's very generous. I'm excited to see her gown."

"Speaking of cocktail gowns, show me yours." Ella stood up. "You said you picked it up in Charleston?"

"I did." Hannah made her way into her bedroom. She turned on the light and then went into the massive walk-in-closet.

She pulled out the garment bag and unzipped it.

"Wow, mom. That's gorgeous. I was expecting something like a red-lace mother-of-the-bride outfit. But this is great! It's fitted which will show off your curves." Ella arched her brow.

"Oh, Ella." She shook her head.

"You still got it so you should flaunt it. Otherwise you'll let yourself go and slide into the muumuu category like Aunt Helen, and won't ever come out of it."

Hannah laughed. "Aunt Helen is perfectly happy with her life. Although it would do her good to get a little more exercise and cut out the Oreos and Netflix." Hannah admitted.

"Believe me, you are still too young to end up like her. You still have a lot of life in you." Ella gave her a pointed look.

Hannah smiled. "Thanks, Honey."

A cell phone dinged. Ella held out her phone and frowned. "It's not mine. Must be yours."

"It's probably Carolina checking on Phoenix."

Ella slid a look at her. "But she just left. Probably hasn't made it to the nursery yet."

Hannah grinned. "She loves that dog more than you know."

"You seem to know a lot about her."

"We've become close. She's divorced and got the lake house in the settlement agreement. It needed a lot of fixing up, but she's come a long way with it. She took on a lot when things were really bad. Carolina's not one to complain but just tackled it head-on."

"Why did she get divorced?" Ella asked.

"Her husband got his twenty-something mistress pregnant." Hannah scowled.

"What a bas… I mean what a jerk." Ella quickly corrected. She shook her head. "So basically she had to start her life all over. That's so sad."

"It is, but she seems really happy with her new life. Carolina has even started dating again."

"Really?" Ella grinned. "Anyone I know?"

"Thomas Harding."

"Nice. I used to have a crush on him when I was a teenager."

Hannah laughed. "Thomas? He's old enough to be your father."

"Mom, he totally looks like a movie star with those brooding good looks." Ella gaped.

Hannah grinned. "I guess I only had eyes for your father."

"Mom, can I ask you something?" Ella walked into the sitting area of Hannah's bedroom and sat in one of the two big chairs that faced the lake.

"Sure, honey." She sat and gave her daughter her undivided attention.

"Have you thought about dipping your toe into the dating waters again?"

Hannah's eyes widened and then she laughed. "Dating? No. I don't think I'll ever be ready to date again."

"I want you to know that when that time comes, I'll be okay with it. I don't want you to stay single because you are worried what Gregory and I will think. I mean, you're still young and a total babe." She reached for her hand.

Hannah arched a brow. "A total babe," she repeated grinning. "Thanks for the compliment, Honey." She squeezed Ella's hand. "Dating isn't even on my radar. And to be honest, it may not ever be. I'm okay with being single."

"You say that now, but give it some time." Ella cocked her head. "Who knows what the future holds?"

Hannah released her hand and stood. "Yes. Who knows? All we have is today. So let's live dangerously. After breakfast let's whip up your favorite gingerbread cookies, and sit by the fire and catch up."

CHAPTER 21

*H*annah finished pulling the cookie sheet of baked cookies out of the oven.

Ella snatched a cookie and played hot potato with it until it cooled down.

"You need to wait until they cool." Hannah shook her head at her daughter's healthy appetite. They'd only finished breakfast half an hour ago. Ella always had a fast metabolism. She would appreciate it when she hit her forties.

"I can't. The smell was making my mouth water. I've had gingerbread cookies at some of the finest bakeries but none compare to yours. You should sell them." Ella took a bite and closed her eyes in appreciation. "So good."

"I know nothing about running a bakery. I bake because I enjoy it. Besides, I might not enjoy it if I was under a deadline."

"I know, I know. Just an idea." Ella snagged two

more cookies and headed into the living room where she had a large glass of cold milk waiting for her. She curled up in the chair by the fireplace and tucked her legs under her. "Hey, Mom, can I give Phoenix a cookie? He's over here begging."

"Should be okay. Just give him one though. I don't want to give him a tummy ache by gorging him on cookies," she called out from the kitchen.

Hannah reached for her phone to check for anymore messages.

She was running out of time. The dedication was only two days away and Fred had not contacted her. If he was indeed the one trying to extort money out of her, then she needed to be ready to send the money when he texted with the account information.

Hannah had debated whether or not to pay the money. After Ella showed up, Hannah realized how much she would do to protect her children. If it got out that James had indeed stolen money, the ramifications would affect both their children and their futures. Ella was doing well in her career as an accountant, but that would change if this got out. Who would hire her then? Gregory was quickly rising in his career and people were now clamoring for his skills. Would they still be seeking him out if this came out? She knew how fickle people could be. One hint of impropriety and they would turn on you. She only had to look at Betty and her gossip about Elena. Paying the money was the only viable option to protect her family and James' reputation.

She'd rather protect her children and their idoliza-tion of their father than to hurt them.

"He's acting funny. I think he needs to go outside."

"I'll take him," Hannah stuck the cookie sheet in the sink to wash when she got back. She grabbed her winter coat and slipped it on. She stuck her phone in the pocket in case she got a call or text.

She found Phoenix's leash and opened the door. "Come on, boy. Let's go outside."

Phoenix cocked his head to the side as if he were comprehending what she was saying and slowly got to his feet. He veered a little but course corrected and headed for the back door.

"Good boy, Phoenix." Hannah stuck the leash in her coat pocket and followed him outside.

Phoenix walked by her side, slow and steady down toward the lake. They stood at the water's edge looking out over the lake.

"Wait up, I want to go, too." Ella called out from the back deck.

Hannah stopped and glanced back up at her daughter who was making her way toward them.

Phoenix let out a bark.

Hannah turned her attention back to the dog.

Two deer had come out from the wooded area beside her house. They stopped when Phoenix barked. Their tails went up and they took off.

Phoenix, forgetting about his stroke, took off after them.

"No, Phoenix, come back!" Hannah yelled and ran

JODI ALLEN VAUGHN

after the dog. If something happened to him, Carolina would be destroyed.

Suddenly her foot caught on something. She heard herself scream as she fell to the ground.

She landed flat on her face, arms outstretched.

"Mom, are you okay?" Ella knelt beside her.

Hannah eased to her knees. "I'm fine. I can't believe how fast Phoenix moved when he saw those deer." She glanced around for the leash.

"I'll go get him." Ella grabbed the leash and ran after the dog.

Hannah got to her feet and shook the snow from her hair. She debated calling Carolina to let her know that Phoenix had gotten away from her. She bit her lip and reached her hand in her pocket to make the call.

"I got him." Ella laughed. "He was waiting on the other side of the wooded area. Think he decided he didn't have it in him to chase them down to the other side of the lake."

Hannah smiled and pressed her hand to her chest. "Thank, God. I don't think I could face Carolina to tell her I lost her dog." She stuck her hand in her pocket. "I was just about to call her."

Hannah frowned.

"What is it?" Ella asked.

"I can't find my phone. It must have fallen out of my pocket when I fell." She looked around in the snow.

"Um, Mom?"

"Yes?"

"I see your phone," Ella cringed. "It fell in the lake."

126

Hannah spun around and saw her phone submerged in the edge of the lake.

"Oh no. My phone." Panic clawed at her throat as her heart thumped loudly.

With her phone out of commission, there was no way to pay the extortioner now.

CHAPTER 22

*H*annah hadn't stopped shaking since Ella helped her inside with Phoenix in tow. Ella had made her sit by the fire while she went over her hands and arms to make sure she hadn't done any serious damage in the fall. Even the dog kept giving her a look of concern with his tilted head.

"Here, drink this." Ella shoved a hot mug of coffee into her hands. "It will help warm you up and stop you from shaking."

"My phone," Hannah blinked. "What about my phone?"

"It's not working. I put it in a Ziplock bag of rice to see if that would help. Honestly, you probably need to get a new one." Ella sat on the arm of the couch.

"Then I need to go to the cell phone store." Hannah stood up, but Ella placed a firm hand on her arm. "No you don't. Besides, they are closed today. I already checked."

"Closed?" Hannah's eyes grew wide.

"Yeah. Due to weather." Ella shrugged. "That's what you get in a small town."

"But I need my phone." Hannah insisted. "What about…what about Albert and the dedication ceremony? What if he tries to call?" Her mind raced. "What if I put my SIM card in your phone?"

Ella barked out a laugh. "And they say my generation is dependent on technology," Ella arched her brow when Hannah didn't join in the joke. "I've already sent a text to Gregory and let him know about your phone. He said he would talk to Albert and let him know in case he has any last-minute changes to the dedication. Also, you can't put your SIM card in my phone. We have different cell phone carriers. It wouldn't work." Ella stood and stretched her back. "If you are okay, I think I'll go lie down for a nap. Getting up at midnight to drive home, has me exhausted."

Hannah nodded. "Yes, go lay down. I'm perfectly fine."

Ella headed to her room leaving Hannah alone with Phoenix. "And stop worrying about your phone," she called over her shoulder.

"What am I going to do now?" Hannah muttered to herself.

Phoenix rested his head on her leg, as if saying he was sorry for the mess he'd gotten her in.

She narrowed her eyes at the dog. "You have any answers?"

Phoenix lifted his head and one ear perked up, as if he were thinking.

With no way to get in contact with her, the extortionist would think she wasn't willing to pay. He would think she was calling his bluff.

She squeezed her eyes shut and tried to think. The doorbell rang. Her eyes sprung open and she stood.

Hannah hurried to the door before whoever was out there could ring the doorbell again. She didn't need Ella coming out to see who it was just in case it might be Fred, coming to get his money.

She opened the door and blinked when she spotted Carolina standing there.

"Oh Hannah. Is everything okay? I tried to call but no one answered. My mind went to the darkest places thinking Phoenix had another stroke and you had rushed him to the vet." Carolina sighed with relief when Phoenix poked his head out behind Hannah's leg.

"Phoenix is fine." She glanced down at the dog. "And I think he's going to make a full recovery, evidenced by the fact he took off chasing some deer this morning by the lake." She held the door open so Carolina could enter.

"Really?" Carolina stepped inside, smiled, and bent down to pet her dog. "You must be feeling tons better, boy."

"Yeah. I had to chase him and I ended up falling."

Carolina stood up and gasped. "Oh, Hannah. I'm so sorry. Are you okay? Did you get hurt?"

"I'm fine. My phone, on the other hand, fell in the lake." She sighed heavily.

"I'm so sorry. I'll replace it, I promise…"

"I'm not worried about that. What does worry me is that the extortionist was going to text me the account info for me to send the money."

"So you decided to pay." Carolina looked at her without condemnation.

"Yes. I'll pay to protect my children's memory of their father. This would have lasting consequences for them if I don't."

Carolina nodded. "I understand. Have you thought about the fact the person may keep asking for money?"

Hannah nodded. "Yes, I have. But I'll cross that bridge when I get to it."

Carolina frowned. "Did you try putting your phone in rice?"

"Already did that, but it takes about three days. I don't have three days. I even asked Ella if I could put my SIM card in her phone, but we have different carriers, so it won't work."

"What about getting a new phone?"

"My cell phone carrier is closed for a three-day weekend, due to Christmas and inclement weather." She shook her head.

"Walmart isn't closed." Carolina offered.

Hannah jerked her head up. "That's right. They carry cellphones. I forgot." She grabbed her friend by the hands. "You're brilliant."

Carolina blushed. "Well, I wouldn't say that. But I appreciate the compliment. Want me to go with you?"

"Would you? Ella is taking a nap, so now is the perfect time to go before she can ask any questions."

"Let's take my car. That way you can run in while I wait with Phoenix in the car."

"You don't have to go back to work?" Hannah got busy getting her coat and boots on.

"No. Bernice shut the nursery down early. She's been acting funny. Said she was waiting on an important phone call."

"It's that man she met online." Hannah shrugged.

Carolina stared hard. "As much as she talks badly about men, I can't believe she is serious about one."

"You never know, Carolina. People change. Believe me."

CHAPTER 23

"The parking lot is nearly empty." Hannah looked over at Carolina. "Why don't you come in with me? You can bring Phoenix. If anyone asks, say he's a support animal."

"Really? But I thought they were supposed to be wearing a vest?" Carolina looked unsure.

"The worst thing that can happen is they ask you to leave." Hannah looked at her friend and waited for her answer.

"I never pegged you for a rule breaker, Hannah." Carolina unbuckled her seatbelt and turned off her car.

"I've surprised myself these past few days."

They hurried into Walmart as the snow fell around them.

Hannah ran her hand across her hair as soon as she stepped inside. She glanced around. "This place looks deserted."

"I guess everyone has already gotten their bread and

milk in preparation for the oncoming winter weather. The smart people are already at home, safe and cozy by their fireplaces."

"This won't take long. I promise." Hannah walked further into the store and looked at the signs hanging on the aisles. "There." She pointed.

They hurried to the electronic area and found the cell phone booth. The ones like hers were locked up behind the glass counter. Hannah glanced around for a sales associate.

"I'll go see if I can find someone," Carolina volunteered. "Stay here in case someone shows up."

Hannah watched as Carolina and Phoenix walked down the aisle and turned.

"Hannah?"

She turned at the sound of her name. Her face went pale. It was the last person she wanted to see.

"Betty, what are you doing here?" She swallowed hard.

"My sister-in-law is coming for Christmas with her four bratty kids. So I rushed over here to find something to put under the tree." She narrowed her eyes. "They don't really deserve it. The last time they were at our house, they broke the TV while playing indoor football." She shook her head.

"Wow. Maybe they won't be there too long." Hannah bit her lip.

"I'm glad I ran into you. I tried calling you, but it went straight to voice mail."

"My phone fell in the lake."

Betty cringed. "That's awful."

"I'm here to get a new one." Hannah really didn't have time to chitchat with Betty.

Betty stepped closer. "Did you hear about Elena?"

Hannah shook her head. "Betty…"

"She found out about Richard's girlfriend."

"What?" Nausea rolled in her stomach. "How?"

"The mistress called and told her. Richard has denied everything, of course, and she's refusing to believe he's been unfaithful. Turning a blind eye to his unfaithfulness." Betty's mouth curved into a cruel smile.

"Did she tell you this?"

"Of course not. Her maid told my maid. She doesn't want anyone to know. She'd die of embarrassment." Betty laughed.

"That's awful." Hannah's heart hurt for Elena.

"Guess we'll be having our ladies' social at someone else's house. I wouldn't be caught dead over there now." Betty smirked.

Anger flared in Hannah's veins. She fisted her hands at her side. All of the past few days of worry and panic and dread curled itself into a tiny white flame that began to grow deep inside her.

"How dare you."

Betty's smirk quickly melted off her face. "Excuse me?"

"How dare you get enjoyment out of someone's pain? Only a monster would do that."

Betty's lips pressed into a thin line, and she

narrowed her gray eyes. "I would be careful talking to me like that. I have a lot of pull in this town. And you'll be out of the friend circle."

"Perfect. With friends like that, who needs enemies?" Hannah snorted. "Now, if you don't mind." She gave Betty her back.

"I've never been spoken to like that in my entire life." Betty huffed and stormed off toward the paper-goods aisle.

Hannah shook her head. She had just made one more enemy.

Carolina came around the corner with Phoenix in tow. He'd picked up a stuffed penguin and was carrying it in his mouth.

"Did you find someone?"

"Yes, the manager. He told me Phoenix had to go. I told him you wanted to buy a cell phone. He said that the guy who usually works in this section got sick at lunch with the flu. He said that the guy forgot to leave the key to the case and took it home with him. He won't be back to work for at least a week."

"I don't have a week." Hannah squeezed her eyes shut in frustration.

"What if you order one online? Can't they ship it overnight?" Carolina held out her phone. "Here use my phone. I'm going to go pay for this penguin before they call the cops for canine theft."

Hannah nodded. "Yes, go ahead and do that. I'll meet you at the car."

Carolina took off with Phoenix to the front of the

store while Hannah headed for the exit. She stopped in the entrance by the shopping carts and quickly pulled up the type of cell phone she had. She went to order it online but when she went to check out, it said delivery would take a week.

Hannah let out an audible groan. She didn't have a week. She didn't even have a day. Now what was she going to do?

CHAPTER 24

*H*annah glanced back at the cash register at Walmart. Carolina was waiting behind the only other customer in the store.

"I could use some advice, God." Hannah closed her eyes, quietly praying and hoping for a quick answer.

"Hannah?"

Her eyes shot open at the slightly familiar male voice. "Oh, hello. Dr. .."

The doctor on the hospital board gave her a smile. "Dr. Samuels."

"Yes, of course. I'm sorry I didn't remember your name. I was introduced to so many people that night, it was hard to remember them all."

"Completely understandable. I was just stopping in to grab something to cook for dinner tonight." He gave her a strained smile. "I'm not trying to be nosy, but is everything okay?"

Her shoulders slumped and she stared at the

ground. "Ever felt like you did everything in your power to protect someone, and it wasn't enough?"

"Yes."

She jerked her head up to him. "Really?"

He nodded. "A couple of years ago, I got called in to the hospital for an emergency surgery. A young female had been in a car accident and it caused her aorta to dissect. I did everything in my power to save her life but even my most valiant effort wasn't enough."

"I'm sorry. That must have been hard."

"It was. You see, she was my sister."

Her hand flew to her mouth. "Dr. Samuels, I had no idea."

"It's not something you bring up when you first meet someone. Kind of a conversation killer, don't you think?" He smiled, yet she could see that pain lingered in his eyes.

"How did you survive that?" What she was going through paled in comparison to his tragedy.

"It took me a long time to get over that night. But I had to come to terms with the fact that despite doing my best, I am still not in control. I believe that God gives us all a specific number of heartbeats, and when that number is up, it's our time to leave. No matter how hard we fight to control the situation, only One can control life and death. That's God."

"You're right, Dr. Samuels." She nodded slowly.

She'd been trying to control this whole situation instead of trusting. A lot of things could happen between now and the dedication ceremony. Her phone could miraculously start working. Her extortioner might get some Christmas spirit and change his mind. The dedication ceremony might even get cancelled due to this weather.

She had to stop trying to control this situation and trust that whatever was going to happen, was going to happen for a reason.

She'd deal with the fallout later.

"Please, call me John." He looked out at the parking lot covered in snow. "You really should be getting home. The forecast is calling for freezing rain. I wouldn't want you to get stranded."

Hannah nodded. "I was just waiting on a friend to check out. We are headed straight home."

"Good." He cocked his head. "Forgive me for being so forward, but are you sure there isn't anything I can do for you? You looked pretty upset when I walked up."

"I was upset. But after talking to you, I feel a lot better."

A smile grew on his face. "Good. I'm glad I could help." He ran his hand through his hair. "Anytime you feel like talking, just let me know. I'm a great listener and I make really good coffee."

She blinked at the thought of his offer, and then slowly nodded. "That would be nice."

He gave her one last smile before he walked across the parking lot to his truck.

"Did you order a phone?" Carolina appeared with Phoenix.

"No. I didn't."

Carolina gave her a worried look. "What are you going to do, Hannah?"

"I'm going to go home. Ella is probably worried about where I am, despite me leaving her a note."

The drive home was slow and neither said anything. Phoenix even poked his head in between the seats to rest his head on her shoulder.

She smiled at the comfort the dog was giving her. Maybe she should get a dog. It was something she'd think about after Christmas.

Carolina pulled into her driveway and Ella opened the front door.

"You okay, Hannah?" Carolina asked softly.

"I will be, Carolina. I will be. Right now. I'm going to go inside, soak in the tub, and then go to sleep. If I'm lucky, I'll sleep right through until the New Year. Maybe it will be better than this one."

She slid out of the car and walked up the steps to her house.

"Why didn't you wake me up? I would have taken you to Walmart if you wanted." Ella frowned as Hannah stepped inside the warmth of her house. "Wait, you don't have any bags?"

Hannah stopped and looked at her daughter. "They were out of the one thing I thought I needed. Now I'm going to soak in an Epsom salts bath and lay down. It's been kind of a trying morning."

CHAPTER 25

$\mathcal{H}$annah sat in her chair with her cup of coffee and looked out over the lake.

As much as she wanted to do something, anything, to avoid the consequences of the extortioner, she could do nothing but wait.

Waiting.

It was the hardest thing in the world for Hannah to do.

Weeks of waiting at doctor appointments to get options for James' diagnosis and a plan of care.

Weeks of waiting beside her husband while he received his chemo treatments which would leave him sick and exhausted for days.

Weeks of waiting by her beloved's bedside while he struggled to breath and hang on for her and their children.

She hated waiting.

Hannah took a sip of her coffee as she remembered James' last words to her before he took his final breath.

"I've been blessed beyond my wildest dreams because I had you beside me. You are my greatest treasure."

After the funeral Hannah still found herself waiting. This time, she was waiting for day to fade into night. All she wanted to do was crawl into bed and go to sleep. This went on for months until, finally, her children insisted she visit her family doctor. The doctor confirmed that she was depressed and wanted to start her on antidepressants.

It was then she realized she still had to live her life. Fortified by that realization, she began by setting her alarm every day and rising with the sun. She forced herself to start accepting lunch invitations from her friends and jumped back into her volunteering at the church. At first she hated it. But she knew she still had to carry on, if not for her, then for her kids.

The day she met Carolina, she went over there to confront her about her mailbox which had been hit by Carolina's renters. It irritated her that compensation had never been made and, well frankly, she'd gotten some of her gumption back. Or, maybe it was misplaced anger. She wasn't sure. All she knew is that she expected at least an argument out of Carolina.

Instead, she encountered genuine remorse. Hannah found herself lingering at Carolina's house which desperately needed repairs. Hannah had been shocked when Carolina shared her recent divorce and how she'd found out her husband had been cheating.

Hannah had never met anyone who was such an open book.

It was refreshing.

By the time she left Carolina's, she found herself smiling, something she'd not done in a long while.

She took another sip of her coffee and shook her head. Carolina was a special person. She was lucky to call her friend.

"You're up early." Gregory walked into the living room and sat in the chair across from her. "I expected you would be sleeping in since we stayed up playing board games last night."

Gregory and Shelia had arrived the same day Hannah and Carolina went to Walmart. They wanted to arrive before the weather conditions got worse. Hannah was grateful. With her children back in the house, she could put all her focus on them and Shelia.

"I'm used to getting up early. I find if I oversleep then I feel like I've missed half the day. How did you and Shelia sleep?"

"I slept wonderfully. I'm assuming Shelia did too because she was still sleeping when I got out of the shower."

"Good. Want me to get you a cup of coffee?"

"I'll get one in a minute. I wanted to talk to you before the girls got up. It seems like we've not had a minute alone."

"Okay, honey. What do you want to talk about?" She smiled and gave her full attention to her son.

"I want to talk about those...letters." Gregory's expression grew serious.

She sighed heavily. This conversation was bound to come. She simply was not ready. Frankly, she'd never be ready to talk about James and this mess with her kids. It was her job to protect them. Lately, she found herself failing that goal on every front.

"Did you take them to the police?" He studied her.

"No, I haven't," she admitted. She held up her hand. "And before you start lecturing, let me just tell you that I've not gotten any more."

"Good. Maybe whoever it was got scared and stopped."

She doubted the notion, but wasn't going to tell Gregory that.

"Ella said she tried to take you to buy a gun."

Hannah rolled her eyes.

"It's not a bad idea, you know." Gregory rested his arms on his knees and interlocked his fingers together. "You are alone in this house."

"I'll get a dog before I get a gun." Hannah crossed her arms over her chest.

"A dog?" Gregory looked at her like she'd lost her mind.

"I've dog sat Carolina's dog, Phoenix. I can handle a dog."

"Yeah, I heard. You fell and dropped your phone in the lake."

She lifted her chin. "But I didn't lose the dog, did I?"

A slow grin spread across his face. "No, I suppose you didn't."

"Let's change the subject, shall we? Is your tux ready to go for tonight's events?"

"Yes, it's ready. Are you nervous about tonight?" Gregory leaned back in the chair and looked out at the lake. The sun was rising and casting its rays across the water making it sparkle like diamonds.

"A little," she admitted. "I'm sure it will be a night to remember." Truth be told, she was a lot nervous. But there was nothing she could do about it now. She just had to wait.

CHAPTER 26

*H*annah applied her favorite red lipstick and stood back and looked at her reflection in the mirror.

"Perfect," she murmured. The shade matched her dress, which fit perfectly.

She smiled. James would have loved to see her in it. She swallowed and shoved back her emotional thoughts.

So much had changed. Not only was James no longer with her, but his reputation was in question.

Tonight, he would be honored. Was he even who everyone thought he was? Did she even know him at all?

"Now is not the time for tears, Hannah," she reminded herself, dabbing at her eyes so her makeup wouldn't smudge. She walked over to the bed and picked up her faux-fur cape that James had given her when they were on vacation in Iceland.

"Mom, your friend is here." Gregory called out from the living room.

Hannah grabbed her clutch and cape.

When she stepped into the living room, she did a double take.

"Carolina, you look stunning." Hannah smiled at her friend.

Carolina blushed. "Thank you. It's been a while since I had an occasion to dress up." She walked over to Hannah. "Hannah, you look…wow." She scrambled for the right words.

"You look like you stepped off a runway." Carolina finally said.

"That's what I've been telling her." Ella came into the living room.

"And Ella, you look like a model. You've got good genes, honey." Carolina nodded.

"Thank you." Ella beamed at Carolina's compliment.

"You didn't have to offer to let me ride with you guys. I could have taken my car." Carolina looked at Hannah.

The doorbell rang.

Hannah grinned and looked at her friend. "I have a surprise for you. And I think that might be it."

"A surprise? For me?" Carolina blinked.

"Yes, why don't you go answer the door?" Hannah put her hand on the small of Carolina's back."

Carolina gave her a suspicious look as she made her way to the door. Hannah looked at Ella and nodded.

Ella pulled out her cell phone and turned on the camera.

"I can't imagine what kind of surprise you could possibly have for me on a night like tonight." Carolina shook her head and opened the door. She gasped.

Ella snapped some photos on her phone.

"Wow, Carolina. You look stunning." Thomas Harding stood on the other side wearing a dark suit and tie.

"Thomas. What are you doing here?"

"Can I come in before answering questions?" He grinned.

"Sorry, yes." She stepped back and laughed in spite of herself.

Thomas stepped inside and closed the door behind him. "I'm here because Hannah called and invited me to James' dedication ceremony."

Carolina spun around and grinned at Hannah. "Why didn't you tell me?"

Hannah went over and hugged her friend. "Because I wanted it to be a surprise." She wanted Carolina and Thomas to be as happy as she and James, but she didn't want to embarrass her friend by saying it in front of everyone.

"Now that Thomas is here, we can leave." Hannah wrapped her cape tightly around her.

"You don't mind if Carolina rides with me do you, Hannah?"

"Of course not." Hannah gave Carolina a wink.

Everyone filed out of the house. Carolina reached

for Hannah's hand and gave it a gentle squeeze. "Thank you for inviting Thomas."

"Of course. I wanted him to see you looking beautiful. Besides, Thomas needs to know what a catch he has in you." Hannah winked.

"Thank you, friend." Carolina beamed. Thomas stepped up and held out his arm. She accepted and let him lead her to his truck.

"That was sweet, Hannah." Shelia stepped up to her mother-in-law and gave her a side hug. "Ella told me about Carolina's divorce and everything she's been through. She deserves a happy ending."

Hannah wrapped her arm around her daughter-in-law. "Yes, she does, honey. Now, let's get going."

They drove carefully to the ceremony. The weather over the last few days had caused a lot of traffic issues. This was the first time Hannah had left the house after her failed attempt at Walmart to get a new phone.

While the roads were drivable, there were some dangerous spots on the less-traveled areas.

Gregory had spoken to Albert about the ceremony tonight. He had said due to weather conditions some out-of-town people had to cancel.

He didn't say who, and Hannah hadn't pressed Gregory for answers.

Secretly she hoped that Fred was one of them.

All she knew for sure was she was no longer in control of the situation.

And she never had been.

CHAPTER 27

*H*annah's stomach was in a knot by the time Gregory pulled into the hospital parking lot.

She spent the last few days praying before she went to bed and asking God for advice. Whatever was going to happen tonight she would face head-on.

"I'm letting you ladies out at the door so you don't mess up your heels." Gregory pulled up to the front door and put his Range Rover in park. He slid out of the driver's seat and went around to the passenger's side to open Hannah's door.

Hannah smiled and took her son's hand as she got out of the vehicle. "Thank you, sweetheart."

She pulled her cape tighter around her shoulders and stepped toward the front door of the hospital. What if Fred was already inside, waiting to expose James?

The sliding glass doors slid open and Albert walked out to greet her.

"Hannah, wow you look great!" He grabbed her hands in his and gave her a kiss on the cheek.

"Thank you, Albert. You make that tux look good." She forced a smile and tried to focus on the moment.

He let out a belly laugh. "I had to get a new one. My old one was getting pretty tight around here," he rubbed his large belly.

Ella and Shelia stepped up beside Hannah.

"Albert, you remember my daughter, Ella?" She rested her arm around Ella's waist.

"Ella, wow. You have certainly grown since the last time I saw you." He frowned in thought. "I believe it was your high-school graduation."

"I believe so." She gave him a hug.

"And this is my daughter-in-law, Shelia." Hannah pulled her close.

"It's very nice to meet you, Shelia. I have to say, you all look beautiful." Albert looked over their shoulder. "And Gregory?"

Hannah turned around. "He's parking the car. Here he comes now."

Gregory hurried over to them. "I didn't expect to have trouble finding a parking spot. Sorry for the wait."

"Gregory. You look just like your father. How are you doing?" Albert stuck out his hand.

Gregory smiled at the compliment and shook his hand. "I'm doing really great. Albert, you haven't changed a bit."

Albert laughed and touched his belly. "Just grown a little bit in this area."

They all laughed.

"Let's get inside before everyone freezes." Albert let the ladies and Gregory enter before him.

Hannah was surprised to see they had police standing in full uniform at the elevators waiting for them. Unease clinched around the edges of her heart. Why were they here?

She looked over at Albert.

He smiled. "When the police department heard about the dedication ceremony, they insisted on being represented tonight. James was also very generous to the Fallen Officer Foundation."

Hannah nodded and released the breath she'd been holding. She smiled at each officer before getting on the elevator.

Albert was the last to enter the elevator. He reached over and pushed the button. "I think you'll be really pleased at the turnout. Some people who live out of town called and cancelled due to the weather, but the citizens of Hopeton really turned out."

"That's really amazing, Albert. Thank you for everything you've done." Hannah gave him a grateful smile.

The elevator dinged and the doors flew open. Missy stood there waiting on them.

"Hannah! I was starting to get worried!" She pulled Hannah into a hug the second she stepped out of the elevator.

"Missy," she pulled back and looked at her friend,

"you look lovely." Missy wore a dark plum dress with an overlay of lace that sparkled with sequins.

Missy blushed and grinned. "Thank you, dear. You're very kind. But you, Hannah. You're certainly going to turn some heads tonight."

Hannah shook her head. "I doubt that. Missy, you remember my children, Ella and Gregory? And this is Shelia, my daughter-in-law."

"It's so good to see all of you again." Missy hugged each of them. "Well, let's get inside so you can see what the set-up is like. I'm so excited for you to see how it turned out." Missy led them to the door where two security guards stood on either side. They opened the door for them.

Hannah stepped inside and her mouth dropped. "I wasn't expecting it to be so big."

There was a large stage set up in the front of the room with round tables draped in linen tablecloths and a formal table setting. The room was decorated in festive greenery and silver Christmas colors. Tiny white lights were draped along the walls in a dazzling display.

"We removed the three barrier walls to make it one large space instead of four conference rooms." Missy stepped up next to her and pointed. "And look at the stage, at the large projector screen."

Hannah followed where she was pointing. The projector screen came to life. Pictures of James and her were bigger than life. The photos changed and soon there were old photos of every stage of their life.

Newlyweds, the birth of their children, family vacations, mission trips with their church, Stars Global development.

"How did you get all these pictures?" Hannah's voice broke as she tried to hold the tears back.

"Ella is responsible for that." Missy winked. "I called her as soon as we told you about the dedication ceremony and asked for as many photos as possible. I had no idea she had so many."

Hannah turned to her daughter.

"Shelia helped, too. She went through her wedding album to get me those pictures and I had the rest. Remember when I was going through my scrapbook phase? Well, that's all those pictures. I still haven't finished one scrapbook." Ella sighed.

Hannah hugged her daughter tightly. "I can't believe you kept this a secret from me."

"I wanted this to be a good night for you, Mom." She smiled.

"It is honey, it is." Hannah squeezed her daughter's hand and turned to Shelia. "Thank you for helping, Shelia."

"Of course." She hugged Hannah.

Missy waved over a waiter. He brought over a tray of champagne. "While we are waiting on everyone to arrive, let's have a private toast, shall we?"

Everyone grabbed a flute of champagne.

Albert lifted his glass. "To James, if friendships were gold, he would have been the richest man in the world."

Hannah blinked back the tears and clinked glasses

with everyone before taking a sip of the bubbly champagne.

She sent up a silent prayer for Fred to stay away and not ruin the evening for her kids.

CHAPTER 28

*H*annah nervously watched as the room began to quickly fill up with elegantly dressed people. She searched the crowd for Fred, but thankfully did not find him.

"Missy, where's the bathroom? I should go freshen my lipstick before the ceremony starts." Hannah set her champagne glass down on a table at the back of the room.

"Exit this room and take a left. Go past the elevator and keep going until you see a door on the right marked private. That's the board members' private room where they meet. The bathroom in located inside that." Missy smiled.

"I hope our guests will be able to find it." Hannah laughed.

Missy frowned. "You're right. I'm glad you brought that up. I'll have to get one of the waitstaff to direct people to where the bathroom is."

Hannah nodded and made her way out of the room. She went past the elevators, and according to Missy's instructions, she found the room.

Hannah entered the room, found the light switch and flipped it. The room was bathed in light. It was the same conference room that she and Albert had met in and talked about the dedication ceremony.

Hannah spotted the bathroom at the end of the room. She needed to be quick.

Once inside the bathroom, she shut the door behind her. She found her lipstick and applied it to her lips. Hannah pressed her hand to her trembling stomach and took deep breaths.

She just needed to get through this night unscathed. She would worry about the extortionist tomorrow.

She walked into the boardroom.

The door slowly opened and she smiled. "Ella is that you? Needing the bathroom before the ceremony begins? I told you not to drink all that champagne."

Just then a man wearing a suit stepped inside.

Her smile slid off her face. Nausea washed over her.

Standing in front of her was Fred Sinclair. He was thinner and his hair was starting to recede. Even his suit looked worn. His expression was hard, and it looked like it had been a while since he laughed. The once carefree man she had known, was now someone she barely recognized.

"Hello, Hannah."

She pressed her hand to her stomach to calm her

nerves. She tried to speak, but her mouth had gone dry and her brain seemed to forget how to form words.

"I got your message." He took a step closer.

"My…my message?" Her mind went blank.

"Yes, the one you left in my house when you broke in." He narrowed his eyes.

"I…I…"

"I've been trying to contact you, numerous times, but it went straight to voice mail."

She swallowed hard. "My phone fell in the lake. I put it in rice to try to fix it. But it didn't work. I tried buying a new phone, but I couldn't get one. I even tried to order one online, but it wouldn't be here on time. I did everything in my power to be ready for your call." She seemed to vomit out the words. Once she started talking she couldn't seem to stop.

"I didn't expect you to be here. They said a lot of people cancelled." She added.

"I had to come. I wasn't going to miss this for the world. Wrongs needed to be made right. I'm just sorry it has to be on this night."

Hannah felt her heart squeezed. He was going to destroy James' reputation. She didn't care what people thought about her, but her children would be destroyed. She'd tried everything to protect them and she had failed.

"Hannah, you need to hurry up…" Carolina froze when she spotted Fred in the room with her. "Excuse me. I didn't know you were having a private conversation." She started to step out of the room, but Hannah shook her head.

"No, Carolina. Don't leave. I have no secrets."

Carolina frowned and cut her eyes over at Fred. "I'm sorry. I didn't catch your name."

"Fred Sinclair." He eyed her with suspicion.

Recognition flashed in Carolina's eyes and she looked at Hannah who simply nodded.

"Excuse me, ladies, but…" Dr. Samuels poked his head in the door and stopped. He frowned when he spotted Fred. "Hannah, they want to start the ceremony."

"I'll be there in a minute." Her voice was shaky.

Dr. Samuels nodded but didn't move to leave. "Is everything okay? Would you like me to stay?"

"This is a private matter between me and Hannah." Fred insisted.

Dr. Samuels looked to her when he answered. "Well, I don't feel comfortable leaving you alone with her. I want to hear her tell me to leave. Hannah?"

"Actually, I would like Dr. Samuels and Carolina with me." She lifted her chin. She knew Carolina would stand by her no matter what. She wasn't sure about Dr. Samuels. After tonight he might not want to have coffee with her after all.

"Fine. But close the door. I don't want a bigger audience than what we have." Fred stared at Dr. Samuels.

After the doctor closed the door, he went over to

stand beside Hannah. Carolina was on the other side of her.

"Is everything okay?" he whispered.

"No." She looked up at him. "But I'm going to take your advice. I realize I'm not in control and it's out of my hands. Whatever happens, happens."

CHAPTER 29

*H*annah's arms and legs felt like they weighed a thousand pounds. This was her worst nightmare come to life. Except this time, she wouldn't be waking up.

"I don't especially like having an audience." Fred glared.

"And I don't especially like being blackmailed," she shot back.

"What?" Fred's eyes widened, and he looked from her to Dr. Samuels.

"You know, Fred. From the first letter I received demanding money to keep quiet about James taking money from Stars Global, I was shocked. I couldn't imagine who could be so ruthless to ruin the reputation of a dead man and want money. You were his best friend." She pointed at him, anger rising in her veins. "It has driven me crazy these past few weeks, between the letters and the phone calls, trying to figure out if it was true. And then I found the bank account with a million dollars sitting there. A bank account I didn't haven't any knowledge about." She blinked back tears.

Carolina wrapped her arm around her waist. "You don't have to explain anything to that man."

"Wait, what letters are you talking about?" Fred took a step forward. "And phone calls?"

"The ones that I kept getting in the mail wanting a million dollars to keep quiet about James. And the phone call telling me to get my money together and be prepared to deposit it in an account that you would later provide. The thing is, I never got the call because my phone broke." She wrung her hands together.

"I think I need to go get security." Dr. Samuels looked at her.

"Yes, that might be for the best." Hannah acknowledged.

Dr. Samuels started for the door and stopped beside Fred. "I can be in the room in less than a minute. So don't you even dare think about trying anything."

"I've got her covered," Carolina pulled a butter knife out of her clutch.

"Carolina," Hannah gasped. "What are you going to do with that thing?"

"I took it off the table when I came looking for you. I wanted to be prepared for anything." She held the knife up for Fred to see. Dr. Samuels nodded and hurried out the door.

Fred held up his hands. "I think there has been a

terrible misunderstanding. First of all, I would never hurt you, Hannah."

"Oh yeah, then why did you try to extort money from her?" Carolina pierced him with a stare.

He frowned and shook his head. "I didn't."

"You didn't?" Hannah's breath slowly left her lungs. She felt oddly relieved.

Fred slumped down into one of the chairs. "No Hannah. I'm sorry that you would ever think I would do something like that."

"But you left Stars Global and moved away from North Carolina. Didn't you leave because you found out that James took money from the company?"

"No, Hannah. I left because James found out *I* was taking money from the company. It came to a million dollars." He scrubbed his hand across his face. "When James found out he was livid. But mostly I think he was hurt that I had done that."

Hannah shook her head. "You took the money? But why?"

He sighed heavily, like a man who had the weight of the world on his shoulders. "Because I had a gambling problem. I had lost most of my money and thought I could turn it around if I just had one big win. So, like a crazed idiot, I took money from the company."

"Isn't that embezzlement?" Carolina cocked her head.

"Actually, it's misappropriation of funds. Since we owned it." He shook his head. "I lost that money, too. That's when James found out. He offered to pay for me to go to rehab for my addiction. I said no. I denied I had a problem. He told me he didn't trust me. He said if I resigned and relocated to another town, without causing a scene, he would give me a good severance package. He made good on his promise. I moved to Charleston to a house I couldn't afford and ended up having to sell it. I had to hit rock bottom before I could start to climb out of the hole I had dug for myself. I moved to Charlotte and got into a house I could afford and began a Twelve-step program at a church I started attending. I emailed him and told him I wanted to pay back the company. In an unexpected revelation, James told me he put the money back out of his own savings account. So, I told him to open a separate account and I would deposit what I owed him. We agreed to keep our arrangement quiet."

"How did you get that much money?" Carolina crossed her arms, clearly not believing anything that came out of his mouth.

"As luck would have it, my uncle died. Left me a mighty hefty inheritance. So I immediately deposited what I owed James in that account." He shook his head. "It wasn't long after that, James was diagnosed with cancer. I'm thinking he probably never had a chance to move the money into your savings account before he…" his voice cracked as his face filled with emotion.

"I don't understand. If you aren't the one sending the letters or calls, then who is?" Hannah frowned.

Suddenly out of the shadows Terri appeared. "It wasn't Fred. It was me."

CHAPTER 30

*H*annah's breath caught in her throat. Terri, wearing a long black dress with a revealing slit up the side, stepped up beside Fred and reached for his hand.

He snatched it away and stared at her in disbelief. "Terri? You've been trying to blackmail Hannah?"

"Yes." She looked at Fred and let out a cackle. "I did it for you."

"For me?" He stepped back from her.

Terri smiled and turned her attention to Hannah. "James found out about me and Fred dating. He said it couldn't go on. Our relationship broke the company's 'no nepotism policy'. He said if we didn't break it off then one of us would need to terminate our relationship with the company. Well, we broke it off and he still made Fred leave. What he didn't know was I noticed money missing from the account when I was doing the bookkeeping." She pressed her lips into a thin white line.

"Wait, you and Fred?" Hannah looked between them.

"It's not like it was a serious relationship." Fred shook his head. "We were at a convention and I got drunk one night. We ended up spending the night together. I confessed it to James and he told me to break it off. I did. It was a one-time thing."

Terri's eyes widened. It was clear that she was hurt by his confession.

Carolina leaned toward Hannah and whispered. "Must have been a lot of alcohol involved."

"So, if you thought James made Fred leave over you, then why didn't you send him the threatening letters instead of Hannah?" Carolina frowned.

"I did. James never responded to my threats. And he had the audacity to die." Terri looked put out and she let out a cackle. "So I was forced to wait until a more opportune moment arose. A widow is most vulnerable during the holidays."

"You're crazy. I can't believe you did this to Hannah." Carolina cringed.

"And she better pay up or I'm going to let everyone know James stole company money." Terri's eyes sparkled with unhinged delight as she let out another cackle.

"You idiot." Carolina barked out a laugh. "It wasn't James that stole the money. It was Fred."

Terri laughed and looked at Fred who simply

nodded. "That can't be right. You left. You were forced out because we couldn't be together."

"I terminated with the company and left because James found out I was stealing money. I didn't leave because of you. What happened that night between us was a horrible mistake. I'm sorry. It never should have happened. I realized after you tracked me down in Charleston that we would never work out."

"You don't mean that." Terri blinked back tears amidst a nervous cackle. "We had something special."

Hannah noticed movement at the door. Dr. Samuels had appeared with two of the uniformed police she'd spotted at the elevator.

Fred shook his head. "You know, James was right. He told me the love of money is the root of all evil."

"The password." Hannah looked at Fred. "He said that to you?"

"Yes. He said that even if all his money was gone tomorrow he would still be wealthy. Not because of money or material things, but because of his family and friends. I think the real reason James was able to make so much money was because he was generous and kept giving it away." Fred gave a tired smile. "It's a lesson I'm learning."

"So let me get this straight," Hannah turned to Terri and lifted her chin defiantly. "You tried to blackmail me for something James didn't even do."

Terri let out another cackle. "In the end none of this matters. People will still believe what they want to. If you don't pay me that money, I'll post it to every social-

media outlet and news station in North Carolina."
Terri gritted her teeth.

"But that would be illegal. There are laws against blackmail and slander." Hannah crossed her arms over her chest. "There are witnesses. You'd be crazy to try something so stupid."

"Everyone will believe me. These witnesses, as you call them, are all lying to cover up for James and his poor widow. I'm the one they will believe. That's what matters." She cackled again.

"I think the police have heard enough, isn't that right, gentlemen?" Dr. Samuels walked past Terri to stand beside Hannah.

Terri spun around, shocked to see two officers coming towards her.

Dr. Samuels lowered his voice. "I believe your attorney is at one of the tables. I had him stand outside the door listening in, so he could gather the details of what this woman was trying to do to you. So he can advise you."

"Thank you, Dr. Samuels…"

"Please, call me John." He smiled. "I'll take Carolina back to the ceremony, if you want to talk to Fred alone."

"Thank you. I'm sure Thomas is looking for her."

"You sure you don't need me?" Carolina cocked her head.

Hannah smiled. "Thanks for everything you did tonight. Go to the ceremony. I'll be there in a minute."

Hannah went out in the hallway to fill in her lawyer

while the police detained Terri inside the conference room. He advised pressing charges for blackmail and attempted extortion and slander.

When she walked back inside the room, Terri was crying while Fred was looking very uncomfortable at the whole situation.

"Mrs. Reece, we're going to take her down to the station for questioning. We can only hold her for so long unless you decide to press charges."

"I understand. Thank you. I'll let you know."

The officer nodded and led a crying Terri out of the room to the elevators.

"Fred, I owe you an apology."

"For what?"

"For thinking you were the one trying to blackmail me." She shook her head.

"I am surprised you thought I would do such a thing." He shook his head. "Of course, if you really knew what I was capable of…" He let his voice drift.

"Of course ,I believed it was you. Why wouldn't I, given the circumstances?" Hannah sighed. "For starters, you left the company. I thought at first you and James had a falling out, but my husband insisted you didn't."

A ghost of a smile crossed his lips. "James. Always trying to protect my image."

"I tried to find an address for you. I needed to talk to you. I felt like if I could talk to you I would get to the truth. I went to Charleston, but you had moved. And then I went to Charlotte to that house and you were not there."

"I was on a mission trip to help rebuild homes for the tornado victims in Kentucky. Our church started back in the summer sending groups of volunteers out to help. It is an ongoing project."

She smiled. "I never knew you were handy when it came to home construction."

"I'm not. I had to learn while on the job. But it's been good for me. You know, to give back. That's one reason I'm here. I wanted to tell people how good of a person James was. How, even after we went our separate ways, he still checked in on me." Fred looked out the window. "Did you know I came to see him in the hospital?"

"No. I had no idea."

"It happened to be on a day when he was getting chemo."

Hannah frowned. "But I was always here when he had chemo."

"Except for one day." Fred reminded her.

Her eyes widened. "The day my mailbox got hit." She shook her head. "He told me to drop him off at the hospital and run to the hardware store to get a bag of cement. I argued with him but he wasn't having it. I got him up to the chemo floor and then hurried to the hardware store. I ran into one thing after another. They had to get the cement off the top shelf so I had to wait. Then they told me I needed a different bucket to mix the cement in. They had to go find that. By the time I needed to check out I got stuck behind some woman arguing over the price of petunias. Everything took so long that by the time I got back to the hospital, James was done with his chemo treatment."

"We had all the time we needed to talk about forgiveness and moving forward," Fred teared up. "No matter what I did or how I betrayed his trust, James never stopped being my best friend. He never looked at who I'd become. He only saw the pit I'd made of my own life and wanted to reach in and save me...no matter what it cost him personally. Even more, he never told anyone what I did and how I failed him and the company. He kept it between the two of us. I'm blessed because of that."

Hannah blinked back tears. "I'm glad you're here, Fred. James would be proud of how far you've come."

He nodded, too emotional to speak.

A knock at the door caused Hannah to turn.

Dr. Samuels peeked his head in. "I'm sorry, Hannah. But they are ready to start the ceremony. Are you ready?"

She smiled and looked at Fred. "Yes. In fact, I'm more than ready."

CHAPTER 31

*H*annah stepped through the doors into the ceremony.

"Everything okay?" Dr. Samuels appeared at her side.

"Yes, Dr... I mean John. Everything is going to be fine." She smiled up at him.

"Let me escort you to your table. Your children are getting worried about you."

"Thank you, for everything." She looked up at him. "I hope you won't think the worst of me after everything you overheard."

"Are you kidding? A mother who would do anything to protect her children and the reputation of her late husband? You are one in a million." He held out her chair and she sat.

She turned to say something, but he had already headed back to his seat.

"Everything okay?" Gregory leaned over.

"It will be." Hannah looked at him and Ella. "We need to talk when we get home tonight. I have a lot to tell you."

"About what?" Ella looked at her carefully.

"We'll talk tonight. I promise." She patted her daughter's hand. "Tonight is about celebrating your father."

The soft music that had been playing in the background died down as Albert approached the stage. He stepped up to the microphone and smiled.

"Tonight is a very special night. Tonight we are celebrating the life of a man whom everyone called friend. James Reece was taken too soon from us, but he lived a full life with his beautiful wife, Hannah, and two wonderful children, Ella and Gregory. He was generous to a fault and he knew what truly was important in life. We are here tonight to dedicate the children's wing in his honor."

The large screen came to life and showed the new children's wing of the hospital with the new name. James Reece Children's Wing.

Hannah couldn't stop the tears and reached for her napkin. She dabbed at her eyes as the tears flowed.

A loud applause erupted around the room and everyone stood to honor James.

Gregory stood and held out her chair so she could stand.

Hannah rose and felt the arms of her children on either side of her hugging her tight.

When the applause died down, Albert motioned for everyone to sit.

"Now while we are being served, we have a few special guests here tonight who will share with you how much James meant to them."

The wait staff got busy placing their plated food in front of them.

Hannah and her family and friends ate their meal while listening to stories about how James had impacted different people's lives.

Once the speeches were over, they showed the new wing of the children's hospital on the screen. Everyone stood and cheered.

Afterwards everyone was led to the private elevator to go tour the new dedicated wing.

Hannah's eyes misted over as she entered the floor now named after her husband.

Gregory took her hand in his. "What do you think, Mom?"

"There are not enough words to explain how happy I am." She looked up at him and smiled.

He kissed the top of her head. "Dad would probably be embarrassed by all the attention."

"Yeah, he would. But he would be humbled that so many people thought so highly of him." She wrapped her arms around him and hugged him tight.

Albert walked over to them and smiled. "Hannah, I hope you enjoyed the ceremony tonight."

"I did, Albert. It went beyond my expectations. Wonderful job."

"I'm so glad to hear that. James meant a lot to a lot of people." He reached for her hand and gave it a gentle squeeze before heading off to socialize.

"So when were you going to tell us about Terri trying to blackmail you?" Ella stepped up to her and Gregory.

"What?" Gregory pulled away and looked down at Hannah. "Is this true?"

Hannah said, "I'm afraid so." She frowned at Ella. "How did you find out about it?"

"One of the police officers that took her away went to high school with me. He asked if I was alright. I got him to spill the beans."

"Mom!" Gregory looked at her with wide eyes.

"I was going to talk to you and Ella and Shelia tonight after the ceremony. I just didn't want to ruin tonight by bringing it up right now." Hannah cocked her head.

"Fine. Ceremony's over. Let's go back to the conference room upstairs and you can fill us all in." Gregory looked through the crowd and caught Shelia's eye before waving her over.

Carolina walked over to them. "Hannah, I wanted to thank you for inviting me tonight. A touching ceremony as well as some excitement and intrigue." She pulled her butter knife out of her clutch. "I guess I need to put this back before I forget."

Hannah held out her hand. "Here. Let me. I was just about to go upstairs with my children and explain everything that happened."

"Oh, I see. Well, I'll say my goodbyes now." Carolina kissed Hannah on the cheek and said her goodbyes to her children.

"Wait, Carolina knew?" Ella frowned.

"Yes. Why else would she be carrying a butter knife?" Hannah shrugged and headed to the elevator.

She pushed the button and smiled to herself as she left her kids staring after her in bewilderment. "We have a wonderful family, James." She murmured to herself.

A sudden warmth washed over her heart as if he were reaching down from heaven and agreeing with her words.

She squeezed her eyes shut and sent up a silent prayer.

You will always be in my heart. It's time for a new journey with new challenges. And I'll take all the lessons we learned together with me in my new season of life.

Thank you, my love.

"Mom, are you okay?" Gregory stepped up beside her.

"Yes I am, sweetheart. More than you know."

ABOUT THE AUTHOR

Jodi Allen Vaughn is an USA Today best-selling author of over thirty novels. To find her latest release check out her website at http://jodiallenbrice.com

ALSO BY JODI ALLEN VAUGHN

Harland Creek Series

Promise Kept

Promise Made

Promise Forever

Christmas in Harland Creek

Promise of Grace

Promise of Hope

Promise of Love

Laurel Cove Series

Lakehouse Promises

Lakehouse Secrets

Lakehouse Dreams

Stand alone novels.

So This Is Goodbye

Not Like the Other Girls

Harland Creek Cozy Mystery Quilters

Mystery of the Tea Cup Quilt

Mystery of the Drunkards Path Quilt

Mystery of the Grandmother's Garden Quilt

Printed in Great Britain
by Amazon

21415246R00109